You can count on me. *The words echoed in Diana's head.*

"Cam, I really don't need help."

He stared down into her wide eyes. "Yes, you do," he said firmly. "Di, I know you can do this on your own. But since the baby's father isn't around to help you, I'll be around—in case something happens or whatever. You don't have to be alone."

To her horror, her eyes were filling with tears. She fought them back. Tears were a sign of weakness, and she couldn't afford to show that side to anyone. But as she fought for control, he was kissing her lips, moving slowly, touching gently, giving comfort and affection and a sense of protection that left her defenses crumbling.

She swayed toward him like a reed in the wind. He was so wonderful. How could she resist him? A part of her wanted to do whatever he said, anytime, anywhere. And that was exactly the part she had to fight against.

Dear Reader,

Say "California," and most people around the world picture sun-drenched beaches and suntanned bodies, along with movie stars and palm trees. But anyone who has been there knows there is a lot more to California than that. Most of the state is actually rural, and the Central Valley is one huge farm.

And then there is Gold Country—the area where this story is set, and one of the reasons California is called the Golden State. Gold was discovered at Sutter's Mill in 1848, and people streamed in from around the world—by covered wagon, by boat, on horseback—to find their fortune in the hills. A few actually got rich, and some established towns and dynasties along Highway 49 that remain today. It's a beautiful and historic area, far from the coast but just as interesting.

Cameron Van Kirk, the hero of my story, belongs to one of those dynastic families. The heroine, Diana Collins, comes from the opposite extreme— one of the many families who didn't make it rich. I hope you enjoy reading about how they tackle the family obstacles between them and find their way to a loving future.

Regards,

Raye Morgan

RAYE MORGAN

Keeping Her Baby's Secret

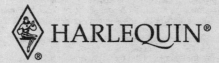

TORONTO • NEW YORK • LONDON
AMSTERDAM • PARIS • SYDNEY • HAMBURG
STOCKHOLM • ATHENS • TOKYO • MILAN • MADRID
PRAGUE • WARSAW • BUDAPEST • AUCKLAND

Recycling programs
for this product may
not exist in your area.

ISBN-13: 978-0-373-17607-6

KEEPING HER BABY'S SECRET

First North American Publication 2009.

Copyright © 2009 by Helen Conrad.

www.eHarlequin.com

Printed in U.S.A.

Raye Morgan has been a nursery-school teacher, a travel agent, a clerk and a business editor, but her best job ever has been writing romances—and fostering romance in her own family at the same time. Current score: two boys married, two more to go. Raye has published more than seventy romances, and claims to have many more waiting in the wings. She lives in Southern California with her husband and whichever son happens to be staying at home at that moment.

Don't miss Raye Morgan's next Harlequin Romance
The Italian's Forgotten Baby
January 2010

This book is dedicated to the Mother Lode and all the wonderful towns along Highway 49.

CHAPTER ONE

DIANA COLLINS woke with a start and lay very still, her heart beating hard in her chest. She stared into the dark room. She'd heard something. She was sure of it.

It was midsummer and her windows were all open. That was nice for ventilation, but not so wise for safety, even out here in the country. Silently she railed at herself. She'd known she should do something about getting bars on the windows or…

But wait. There it was again. The intruder wasn't stumbling around in her little turn-of-the-century cottage. He was still outside. He was…singing.

Slowly she lifted her head. She knew that song. She knew that voice.

"Cam," she whispered, and now a different brand of adrenaline was shooting through her veins. She smiled.

"Cam, you idiot!"

Slipping out of bed, she went to the window and looked down toward the lake. She could just make out a dark figure lounging on the pier. The moonlight glinted on a bottle he was holding as he leaned back to let out a wobbly high note.

"Oh, Cam," she said despairingly, but she was laughing. It must have been ten years since she'd last seen him. Joy flashed through her as she dashed around the room, searching for a robe to throw over her light nightgown—and to conceal, at least for the moment, her rounded belly.

Everything was going to be…well, not okay, but better. Cam was back.

Cameron Garfield Wellington Van Kirk the third was feeling no pain. There was no denying it—he'd been indulging. And since he almost never had more than a single glass of wine at dinner these days, he'd been affected more quickly and more thoroughly than he'd expected. He wondered, fleetingly, why he seemed to be bobbing in a warm, mellow glow. It was unusual, but rather nice.

"Maybe a little too nice," he muttered to himself in a Sam Spade accent, trying to look fierce and world-weary at the same time. It didn't really work. But did that matter when there was no one here to witness it anyway?

Never mind. He was going to sing again. Just one more swig from this nice bottle and he was going to sing that song about Diana.

"'I'm so young, and you're…'" he began tunefully, then stopped, frowning. "Wait a minute. I'm older than she is. This song doesn't make any sense."

An owl called from across the water, then swooped by, its wings hissing in the air.

He turned and there she was, coming down toward the pier, dressed in lacy white and looking like something ethereal, magic—from another world. He squinted, trying to see her better. He wasn't used to thinking of her as part angel, part enchantress. The Diana he'd known was a girl who had both feet firmly placed in a particularly earthy sort of reality. At least, that was the way he remembered it.

"Diana?" he whispered loudly. After all, he didn't want to wake anybody up. "Is that you?"

She came closer and he watched, fascinated, then blinked hard and shook his head. It was his old friend Diana all right but it looked like she was floating. Were her feet even touching the ground? Her cloud of blond hair shimmered around her and the gown billowed in a gust of wind and he felt a catch in his breathing. She was so beautiful. How was it that he'd managed to stay away this long?

"Cam?" she said, her voice as clear as the lake water. "Is that really you?"

He stared at her without answering. "If this is heaven," he mumbled as he watched her, enchanted and weaving dangerously right next to the water, "it's more than I deserve."

"It's Apache Lake, silly," she said as she came onto the pier and headed right for him. "Heaven is still to come."

"For you, maybe," he muttered, shaking his head as he looked her over.

She might look magical but she was all woman now—no longer the barefoot girl with the ragged cutoffs and the skimpy cropped top and a belly-button ring—

and like as not a set of bruises administered by her bully of a father. That was the Diana he'd left behind.

This new Diana was going to take some getting used to. He made no move to give her a hug or a kiss in greeting. Maybe that was because he wanted to with a sudden intensity that set up warning flares. And maybe it was because he'd had too much to drink and didn't trust himself to keep it simple.

"Some of us are still holding our options open," he added irrelevantly.

Her answering laugh was no more relevant, but it didn't matter. She was laughing from the pure joy of seeing him again. She looked up at him, still searching his face as though needing to find bits and pieces of the Cam she remembered. She noted how he was still fighting back the tendency to curl in his almost-black hair. And there were his startlingly blue eyes, crinkling with a hint of laughter. That was still the same. But there was a wary reserve that hadn't been there before. He was harder now, tougher looking. The sweetness of the boy had been sloughed away and in its place there was a cool, manly sort of strength.

For just a moment, her confidence faltered. He was large and impressive in a way she didn't recognize. Maybe he'd changed more than she was going to like. Maybe he'd become someone else, a stranger.

Oh, she hoped not, but her heart was in her throat.

"Hey," he said.

"Hey yourself," she said back softly, her dark eyes luminous in the gloom as she searched for clues in the set of his shoulders, the lines of his face. "What are you doing here?"

He frowned, trying to remember. Everything seemed to have fuzzy edges right now. He'd been on his way home—if you could call the house where his parents and grandfather lived his home. Yeah, that was it. He'd been on his way home, and then, he'd taken a detour….

Suddenly the answer was clear. He'd thought he was just stopping by to say hello to an old friend, putting off the homecoming he had waiting for him at the Van Kirk family mansion on the hill not too far from here. But now he knew there was a flaw in his thinking. There had been another motivation all along. He just hadn't realized it. He'd come to find the person he'd missed most all these years. And here she was, not quite the same, but good enough.

He looked down at her, needing nothing more than the Diana she was today. He soaked her in as though he'd been lost in the desert and dying of thirst. She promised to be something better and more satisfying than mere alcohol could ever be.

They said you can't go home again, and maybe that was true. Things could never be the way they'd been before he left. But that was okay. The way Diana had turned out, things might just be better.

"What am I doing here?" he repeated softly, still struggling with blurry thinking. "Looking for you."

"For me?" She laughed dismissively, looking over his shoulder at the moon. "I think you're looking for someone who isn't here anymore."

"You'll do," he said simply.

They stared into each other's eyes for a long moment, their memories and emotions awakening and connecting in a way their words could never quite explain.

"I thought you weren't ever coming back," she said at last, and her voice had a catch in it that made her wince. Tears of raw feeling were very near the surface and she couldn't let them show. But to see him here, standing on her pier, just as he had in those bygone days, sent her heart soaring.

She looked at him, looked at his open shirt and wide belt, his attractively tight jeans and slim hips, the way his short sleeves revealed nicely swelling biceps and she shook her head. He was so like the young man she'd known, and yet so different. The dark hair was shorter and cut more neatly, though it was mussed a bit now and a spray of it still fell over his eyes, just like always. The face was harder, creases where dimples used to be. But the gorgeous eyes were just as brilliantly blue, sparkling like star-fire in the moonlight.

For so long, she'd been afraid his last declaration to her would come true. Even after all these years, the memory of those final words had the capacity to sting deep down in her heart.

"I'm out of here, and I'm never coming back."

She'd thought her world had melted down that day. And now here he was, back after all.

"Naw," he said carelessly. "I never meant it. Not really."

She nodded. She accepted that. She'd waited for a long time for him to show up again. She'd been so sure he would, despite what he'd said. But after years, when it didn't happen, she'd finally started to lose faith.

She remembered when he'd left. She'd been an angry and confused eighteen-year-old, trapped in a broken home, grasping for a reason to thrive. For so long, he'd been her anchor to all that was good in life. And then he'd left and she'd felt adrift in a world without signs or shelter. She'd been so very all alone.

"What I can't understand is why you're still here," he said.

She lifted her chin. "Where did you think I'd be?"

He shrugged. "I don't know. San Francisco maybe. Becoming sophisticated." He half grinned. "Gettin' swanky."

"Swanky?" She laughed. "That'll be the day."

As if on cue, he began to softly sing the Buddy Holly song of the same name, still staring soulfully into her eyes.

"You're drunk," she accused him, shaking her head as though despairing of him.

He stopped short and grimaced. "No. Impossible." He stared hard, actually trying to convince her. "You can ask anyone. I don't drink."

"Cam!" She looked pointedly at the bottle in his hand.

He looked at it, too, then quickly looked away. "Hey, anyone," he called out a bit groggily across the lake, forgetting all about keeping it quiet. "Tell her. She needs to hear it from a neutral source."

She bit her lip, trying not to laugh at the picture he made. "There's no one out there," she told him simply.

"Sure there is." He turned his heavy-lidded gaze on her. "Look closely, now. Can't you see them?"

Turning to lean on the railing, she looked out across the lake to the stand of pines and cottonwoods shivering in the breeze. It was so good to be here in the night with Cam, almost as though a missing part of her was back in place, where it should be.

"See who?"

"Us." He moved closer and spoke very near her ear. "Cam and Di. The boy and girl we used to be. The ghosts are out there."

She could feel his warm breath on her skin. It made her pulse beat just a little faster and she was enjoying it, for now.

It had been so long.

She'd tried asking about him over the years, first in the village, then at the Van Kirk mansion when she'd been there in connection to her job, and the response she had was minimal. She'd told herself that it looked like he was gone for good, that he'd had some sort of rift with his family that couldn't be repaired—that he was never coming back. She'd tried to convince herself to forget about him. But his influence on her was embedded in her soul. She couldn't shake him loose, no matter what.

And at the same time, she'd always known that she could never really have him. But that was a tragic fact of life, something she'd accepted as a given.

She turned and looked at him. "I don't see anything," she told him, determined to be the realist to his crazy dreamer. "There's nobody out there."

"Sure there is." He frowned as though it was a puzzle that needed solving. "Maybe you should have some of this," he said, brandishing the bottle and looked at her hopefully. "Your vision might get better."

She shook her head, rolling her eyes as she did so. He looked at the bottle, drained it, then frowned, silently reproaching himself. She had a right to hate drinking. She'd certainly suffered enough from the stuff.

"Okay. I'll get rid of it." Easy enough for him to say. The bottle was empty now.

"Wait!" She stopped him from sending it sailing out into the water, snatching it from his hand. "Don't litter in my lake. I'll put it in the trash can."

He blinked at her but didn't protest, leaning back on the railing with his elbows and watching her with the trace of a smile on his handsome face. She tossed the bottle and turned back to him. Her heart lurched at the picture he made in the moonlight, part the man he was now, part the memory of the boy. There had been a time when she would have done anything for him. And now? Hopefully she knew better now.

Looking out across the water again, she pretended to squint and peer into the moonlight. "Wait a minute," she said, looking hard. "I think I see them now. Two crazy kids stomping around in the mud."

"That's them," he said approvingly, then looked down at her. "Or more accurately, that's us."

Us. Yes, they had spent time together on that side of the lake. How could she forget? Some of the best moments of her life had been spent there.

--

Cam was always fighting with his grandfather in those days. After a particularly bad argument, she would often find him down at the far side of Apache Lake, fishing for rainbow trout. She would sit and watch and he would tell her stories about the valley's history or his sister's latest exploit or…sometimes, what he wanted to do with his life. His dreams involved big things far away from gold country. Whenever he talked about them, she felt a sense of sad emptiness inside. She knew she would never be a part of that world.

He always used catch and release, and she would watch regretfully as he threw the shiny, silvery fish back in and they watched it swim away. He didn't realize that she could have used it for dinner. More often than not, the refrigerator at her house was bare and her father was off somewhere burning through the money that should have gone to food, pouring it down his throat in the form of bargain wine. But she never said a word to Cam. She was too embarrassed to let him know her dinner would be a cheap candy bar that night.

Such things were not a problem any longer. She had a nice little business that kept her comfortable, if not exactly rolling in wealth. These days she was more likely to try to cut down on calories than to need to scrounge for protein.

Times had changed. She'd traded a rough childhood for an adulthood that was a lot nicer. She'd been a damaged person then. She was okay now.

Her hands tightened on the railing and she bit down on her lower lip to keep it from trembling. Who was she trying to kid? A woman who was content with her life didn't take the steps to change things that she had recently done.

He hadn't noticed yet. She resisted the urge to pull her robe more carefully over her slightly rounded belly. He was going to have to know the truth some time and it might as well be now.

Well, maybe not now. But very soon.

"Remember the night before I left?" he was saying, his voice low and slightly hoarse. "Remember...?"

He let his voice trail off and she closed her eyes. She remembered all right. She would never forget. It was the one and only time he'd ever kissed her. It wasn't much of a kiss—not at all the kind of kiss she'd yearned for. His lips had barely touched hers. But she still considered it the best kiss she'd ever had.

She felt him touching her hair and she sighed. If she turned to look at him, would he kiss her again? She tried it, moving slowly, opening her eyes to look up into his face. For just a moment, she thought he might do it. But then a look of regret came into his eyes and he turned from her, moving restlessly.

Her heart sank, but she scolded herself at the same time. What was she thinking? A romance with Cam was not in the cards—never had been.

"So where have you been all this time?" she probed to get her mind on other things.

He shrugged. "Pretty much everywhere. Served a few years in the Navy. Worked on an oilrig in the Gulf. Spent some time as a bodyguard in Thailand. The usual stuff."

She nodded. This was definitely not the sort of thing his mother would have bragged about. If he'd been at law school on law review, spent time working as an aide to the governor, or made a pile of money on Wall Street, she would have made sure the local paper covered it in minute detail. Cam had always had a tendency to turn away from the upper class path to respect and follow his own route to…what? That had often been a bone of contention between him and his family.

But who was she to complain? It was exactly that inclination that had led him to be her protector for those early years. Their friendship had started when she was in Middle School. Her father was the town drunk and that meant she was the object of vile names and other indignities that adolescent boys seemed compelled to visit upon those weaker than themselves. Cam was a couple of years older. He saw immediately what was going on in her life and he stepped in to make it stop.

That first time had been like magic. She'd gone for a swim at the park pool. None of her friends had shown up and suddenly, she'd been surrounded by a group of boys who had begun to taunt her, circling and snapping at her like a pack of wolves. She knew she could hold her own against one boy, or even two or three, but there were too many this time and she panicked. She tried to run, which only egged them on, and just when she thought she was going to be taken down like a frightened deer, Cam appeared on the scene.

He was only a few years older than the boys, but his sense of strength and authority gave him the upper hand

and they scattered as soon as he challenged them. He picked her up, dusted her off and took her for ice cream. And that began a friendship that lasted all through her school years. He was her protector, the force behind the calm, the one who made everything okay.

Even when he'd gone away to university, he'd checked on her whenever he came home. He treated her like a big brother. The only problem was, she'd never been able to completely think of him that way.

No, from the start, she'd had a major crush on him. It hadn't been easy to hide. And the effects had lingered long after he'd skipped town and left her behind. In fact, she knew very well it was her feelings for him that had ruined every relationship she'd attempted ever since.

"So you've pretty much been bumming around the world for ten years?" she asked, frowning as she looked at him again. Whatever he'd been doing, it actually looked to be profitable. Now that she noticed, his clothing was rumpled, but top-of-the-line. And that watch he wore looked like it could be traded in for a down payment on a small house.

"Not really," he told her. "The first five years, maybe. But then I sort of fell into a pretty lucrative situation." He shrugged. "I started my own business in San Diego and I've done pretty well."

"Good for you."

He shrugged again. "I've been lucky."

She knew it was more than that. He was quick, smart, competent. Whatever that business was, he was evidently successful at it.

"And all that time, you never thought a simple phone call might have been in order?" she asked lightly. "A letter, maybe? Just some sign that you were still alive and well?"

She bit her lip again. Was she whining? Better to drop it.

He shook his head. "I figured a clean break was the best way," he said softly.

She winced. That was exactly what he'd said that night, after he'd kissed her. But she wasn't going to complain anymore. It wasn't like he owed her anything. When you came right down to it, he'd done more for her than anyone else ever had. What more could she ask for?

That was a dangerous question and she shied away from it quickly.

"So what brought you back?" she asked. "Are you back for good?" The words were out of her mouth before she could stop them and she made a face, knowing she had sounded altogether too hopeful.

He looked at her, then at the moon. "Hard to tell at this point," he muttered. Turning, he looked back toward the little house she lived in. She'd done something to it. Even in the dark, it didn't look so much like a shack anymore.

"Your old man still around?" he asked.

"He died a few years ago," she told him. "Complications from pneumonia."

Complications from being a rotten drunk was what she could have said, he thought bitterly. She was better off without him. But that being said, you didn't get to choose your relatives and he *was* her father.

"Sorry," he muttered, looking away.

"Thanks," she said shortly. "For all the grief he gave me, he did manage to hang onto this little piece of property, so it's mine now. All five acres of it."

He nodded, then smiled, happy to think of her having something like this for her own. Whenever he'd thought of her over the years, he'd pictured her here, at the lake. It was so much a part of her.

"I had a funeral for him," she went on. "At the little chapel on Main. I thought it would just be me and him." She shook her head, remembering. "Do you know, most of the town came? I couldn't believe it." She grinned. "I even had a cousin I'd never met before show up, Ben Lanker. He's an attorney in Sacramento and he wanted to go over the will for me, to see if all was okay." She laughed shortly. "I think he was hoping to find a flaw, to see if there was some way he could get his hands on this property. But I'd had everything nailed down clear and legal when I was dating a lawyer in San Francisco, so he was out of luck."

He laughed along with her, pleased to know she was taking care of herself these days. Looking at her, he couldn't imagine her being a victim in any way.

"So tell me, Cam," she said. "The truth this time. I'm still waiting to hear the answer to my question. What brings you back to your ancestral home?"

He sighed. "It's a fairly easy answer. I'm just embarrassed to tell you."

That made her laugh again. "Oh, now I *have* to hear it. Come on. The raw, unvarnished truth. Give it up." She smiled at him. "What did you come home for?"

Giving her a sheepish look, he grimaced.

"Okay. You asked for it."

She waited expectantly. He took a deep breath, as though this was really tough to admit.

"I came home to get married."

CHAPTER TWO

THE smile froze on Diana's face. She blinked a few times, but she didn't say anything. Still, it felt as though Cam had shot an arrow through her heart.

It shouldn't have. She had no right to feel that way. But rights didn't wait on feelings. She stared at him, numb.

"Married!" she finally managed to say in a voice that was almost normal. "You?"

He coughed discreetly. "Well, that's not actually technically true."

She blinked. "Cam!"

One dark eyebrow rose provocatively. "Take it as a metaphor."

"A metaphor!"

He was driving her crazy. She shook her head. It was too early in the morning for mind games.

"Will you tell me what is really going on?"

He sighed. "Let's just say my mother has plans. She thinks it's time I settled down."

"Really." Diana took a deep breath. So…was he getting married or wasn't he? She was completely confused and beginning to get annoyed. "Who's the lucky girl?"

He looked at her blearily. "What girl?"

She wanted to throw something at him and it took all her strength not to snap back through clenched teeth. "The girl your mother wants you to marry."

"Oh." He frowned as though he didn't see how this mattered. "There's no specific girl. More like a category of women." He shrugged and raked fingers through his tousled hair, adding to his slightly bewildered look. "She has a whole roster picked out. She's ready to toss them at me, one at a time, and I'm supposed to catch one of them in the end."

Diana took a deep breath. This had been the most maddening conversation she'd had in a long time. The strongest impulse she had right now was to push him into the lake. How dare he come back here this way, raising old emotions, raising old hopeless dreams, and then slapping her back down with vague news of pending nuptials? Was this a joke? Or was he just trying to torture her?

But she knew that wasn't really it. He didn't have a clue how she had always felt about him, did he? Well, despite the position it put her in, that was probably a good thing.

Holding all that in as best she could, she looked out at the moonlight on the lake. Funny. Cam had come home and within minutes she had reverted back to being the little raggedy urchin who saw him as her white knight. For years she'd clung to his protection, dreaming that one day, when she was older, he would notice that she wasn't a little girl anymore, that she'd grown into a woman.

She sighed softly. It had always been a stupid goal, and still was. He was from a different world and only visited hers when it suited him. He wasn't available, in other words. And even if he were, what she'd done to her own situation alone would rule out any hopes she might have. She should know better by now. A little toughness of her own was in order. No more shabby girl with her nose pressed to the windowpane.

She tilted her head to the side, a bemused look on her face as she worked on developing a bit of inner strength.

"Let me get this straight," she challenged. "You came back because your mother wanted you to?"

He blinked at her groggily. "Sort of," he admitted.

She shook her head, eyes flashing. "Who are you and what have you done with the real Cam Van Kirk?" she demanded.

"You don't buy it, huh?" He looked at her, trying to be earnest but too groggy to manage it well. The swath of dark hair that had fallen down over his eyes wasn't helping. He was looking more vulnerable than she'd ever imagined he could look.

"Actually," he murmured, "neither do I."

"What does that mean?"

"Come on, Di, you know how it is. You grow up. You begin to realize what is really important in life. And you do things you never thought you would."

Sure, she knew how it was. But she couldn't quite believe it. Not Cam. Not the young rebel she'd idolized for so many years.

"What happened to you, Cam?" she asked softly, searching his face.

He moved toward her, his hand reaching in to slide along her chin and cup her cheek. She pulled back, looking surprised at his touch and pushing his hand away.

And as she did so, she forgot to hold her robe closed and it fell open. Her rounded belly was obvious.

"Whoa," he said, jerking back and staring at it, then looking up at her face. He shook his head as though trying to clear it so that he could deal with this new development. "What happened to *you?*"

"It's not that big a mystery," she said quickly, pulling the robe back. "It happens a lot, in case you hadn't noticed."

He stared at her for a moment, his brow furled, and moved a bit further away, purposefully keeping his eyes averted from her midsection.

"Did you go and get married or something?" he muttered uncomfortably.

She looked away and he frowned. The downside of that possibility was suddenly clear to him. He didn't want her to be married. Given a choice, he would rather she wasn't pregnant, either. But that was clearly settled and he could have no influence on it. But the married part—no, if she were married he was going to have to leave pretty quickly and probably not come back.

Why hadn't he considered this possibility? Somehow it had seemed natural to find her here, just where he'd left her. But of course things had changed. It had been ten years, after all.

"No, Cam," she said calmly. She pulled the robe in closer and looked out at the lake. "I'm not married."

Was he supposed to feel relief at that? Probably not. It was pretty selfish of him. But he couldn't help it. Still, it left a few problems behind. There had to be a man involved in this situation. Cam blinked hard and tried to act sober.

"Who's the daddy? Anyone I know?"

She shook her head. "It doesn't matter."

He shrugged. "Your call. So I guess you're doing this on your own, huh? Are you ready for that?"

She gave him a quick, fleeting smile. "I'm fine, Cam. I can handle this."

Something stirred inside him. Was it admiration? Or regret? He was a bit too groggy to tell. But the Diana he'd left behind had seemed to need him in so many ways. This one, not so much. That was probably a good thing. Wasn't it? If only he could think clearly, he might even be able to tell.

"Well, you know, if you need any help…" he began.

She turned on him, ready to be defensively self-reliant, and that was when she saw what looked like blood. It was trickling down out of his dark hair, making a rivulet in front of his ear. She gasped, then looked more closely, detecting a lot more that had started to dry against the collar of his shirt.

"Cam! What's this?" She touched it and showed him.

"Oh, just a little blood." He pulled out a handkerchief and dabbed at it.

"Blood!"

He gave her a melancholy smile. "I had a little accident. Just a little one."

She stared. "With your car?"

He nodded. "The car wouldn't go where I tried to get it to go. I kept pulling on the wheel and saying, 'Come on, car, we've got to get to the Van Kirk mansion,' and the stupid car kept saying, 'You know you'd rather go see Diana.'" He looked at her with mock earnestness. "So we crashed." He waved toward the woods. "We smashed right into a tree."

"Cam!"

"Just a little one. But I hit my head pretty hard. Didn't you hear it?"

She stared at him, shaking her head. "Oh, Cam."

"It wasn't very far away." He frowned. "I'm surprised you didn't hear it."

"I was asleep."

"Oh." He sighed and stretched out his arms, yawning. "Sleep, huh? I used to do that."

She noticed the dark circles under his eyes. For all his handsome features, he did look tired. "Maybe you shouldn't drink when you drive," she pointed out sharply.

"I didn't." He shook his head. "The drinking came later."

"Oh."

He shrugged. "Just a bottle I found in the trunk after the crash. I brought it along to tide me over while I waited on your pier for the sun to come up." He looked forlorn. "I was planning to invite myself for breakfast."

How did he manage to look so darn lovable in this ridiculous state?

"It's still a little early for breakfast." She sighed, then reached out and took his hand. "Come on."

"Okay," he said, and started off with her. "Where are we going?"

"Where else would the prodigal son go? I'm going to take you home."

The drive up to the Van Kirk mansion was steep and winding. Diana had made it often over the last few years in her little business van. Alice Van Kirk, Cam's mother, had been one of the first people to hire her fledgling floral styling company to provide fresh arrangements for the house once a week back when she'd originally started it.

The sky had begun to lighten, but true dawn lurked at least a half hour away. Still, there was enough light to let her see the turrets and spirals of the Van Kirk mansion ahead, reaching up over the tops of the eucalyptus trees, shrouded in the wisps of morning fog. As a child, she'd thought of the house as an enchanted castle where royalty lived high above the mundane lives of the valley people, and it looked very much like that now.

"Are they expecting you today?" she asked.

When she didn't get an answer, she glanced at Cam in the passenger's seat. He was drifting off to sleep.

"Hey!" She poked at him with her elbow. "I don't think you should let yourself sleep until you see a doctor. You might have a concussion or something."

"Hmm?" he responded, looking at her through mere slits where alert eyes should be.

"Cam, don't fall asleep," she ordered.

"Okay," he said, and his eyes immediately closed all the way.

"Oh!" she said, exasperated and poking him with her elbow again. "Here we are. Which door do you want?" She grimaced. "I don't suppose you have a key, though, do you?"

He didn't answer and his body looked as relaxed as a rag doll. With a sigh, she pulled into the back entrance, using the route she was used to. The servants' entrance she supposed they probably called it. The tradesmen's gate? Whatever, it was just off the kitchen and gave handy access to the parts of the house where she brought flower arrangements once a week. She rarely ran into any of the Van Kirks when she came. She usually dealt with Rosa Munez, the housekeeper. Rosa was a conscientious employee, but she doubted the woman would be up this early.

"How am I going to get you in there?" she asked, shaking her head as she gazed at the dark house. Turning, she reached out and pushed his dark hair back off his forehead. His face was so handsome, his features so classically perfect. For just a moment, she ached, longing to find a place in his arms. But she couldn't do that. She had to be tough.

"Cam," she said firmly, shaking his shoulder. "Come on, wake up."

"Okay," he murmured, but his eyes didn't open.

This made things a bit awkward.

Slipping out of the car, she went to the door and looked at the brass handle, loath to try it. She knew it would be locked, and she assumed there was a security system on the house. Everyone was obviously still asleep. What the heck was she going to do?

Stepping back, she looked up at the windows, wondering if she could climb up and get in that way, then picturing the embarrassment as she hung from a drainpipe, nightgown billowing in the breeze, while alarm bells went off all through the house. Not a good bet.

Turning, she went back to the car and slid into the driver's seat.

"Cam, I don't know what we're going to do," she said.

He was sound asleep and didn't even bother to twitch. She sighed with resignation. She was going to have to wake up the whole house, wasn't she? Now she regretted having come without changing into day clothes. But she hadn't been sure she could keep Cam in one place if she left him to go change, and she'd thought she would just drop him at his doorway and make a run for home. She should have known nothing was ever that easy.

"Okay. If I've got to do it, I might as well get it over with," she said, leaving the car again and going back to the door. Her finger was hovering half an inch from the doorbell and she was bracing for the sound explosion she was about to unleash on the unsuspecting occupants, when the door suddenly opened and she found herself face-to-face with Cam's sister, Janey.

"Diana? What in the world are you doing here?" she demanded.

"Janey!" Diana was immediately aware of how odd she must look standing on the Van Kirk doorstep in her filmy nightgown and fluffy white robe. The shabby slippers didn't help, either.

Janey, on the other hand, looked trendy and stylish in high end jogging togs. A tall, pretty woman about a year younger than Diana, she was evidently up for an early morning run and determined to look chic about it. Diana couldn't help but have a quick catty thought wondering which of the local squirrels and chipmunks she might be trying to impress. But she pushed that aside and felt nothing but relief to have a member of the family appear at the door.

She and Cam's sister had known each other forever but had never been friends. Janey had been aware of the close ties between Diana and her brother, and she'd made it very clear in very public ways that she didn't approve. But that was years ago. When they saw each other now, they weren't exactly warm, but they were perfectly civil.

"Janey," Diana said, sighing with relief. "I've got Cam in the car. He was in an accident."

"What?"

"Not too bad," she reassured her quickly. "He seems to be basically okay, but I think a doctor ought to look him over. And...well..." She winced. "He's been drinking so..."

"You're kidding." Janey followed her to the car and then they were both fussing over her brother.

"Cam, you blockhead, wake up," Janey ordered, shaking his shoulder. "We haven't seen you in years and this is the way you arrive?"

He opened one eye. "Janey? I thought I recognized your dulcet tones."

She shook her head. "Come on. I'll help you up to your room. I'm sure Mother will want to call Dr. Timmer."

"I don't need Dr. Timmer," he grumbled, though he did begin to leverage himself out of the car. "If Diana can take care of herself, I can take care of myself." He tried to pound his own chest and missed. "We're a pair of independents, Diana and I."

Janey gave him her arm and a quizzical look. "I have no idea what you're talking about," she said crisply. "Come on. We'll let your friend get back to her…whatever."

"Diana is my best friend," he murmured, sounding almost melancholy. "My favorite person in this valley. Always has been."

Janey chose that moment to notice Diana's baby bulge. Stopping short, she gasped. "Cam! Oh, no!"

Despite his condition, he immediately recognized the way her mind was trending and he groaned. "Listen, Janey, I just got into town at about 2:00 a.m. Not even I could get a lady with child that fast."

"*Humph*," she harrumphed, throwing Diana a look that took in everything about her pregnancy and the fact that she was running around the countryside in her nightgown, delivering a rather inebriated Cam to his old homestead. It was obvious all this looked pretty darn fishy to her.

Diana almost laughed aloud. If Janey only knew the irony involved here. "Can you handle him without me?" she asked the other woman. "I'd like to get home and try to get some sleep. I do have an appointment back here with your mother at eleven."

"Go, go," Janey said, waving a hand dismissively and turning away.

But Cam didn't turn with her. He stayed where he was, looking back at Diana. "I was just getting used to having you around again, Di," he said. "A little later, when I've had some sleep…"

"You'll be busy getting caught up on all the family news," Janey said quickly. "And learning to give up living like a drifter."

"Like a drifter?" Cam looked up as though that reminded him of something and Diana laughed.

"Watch out, or he'll break out into song on you," she warned his sister as she turned for her car. As she walked away, she heard the Cam's voice warbling, "'Here I go again…'" She grinned.

Cam was back. What did this mean? Right now, it meant she was full of sadness and happiness at the same time.

"The thrill of victory and the agony of defeat," she murmured nonsensically as she began the drive down the hill. A moment later, tears were streaming down her face and she had no idea why.

But Cam was back. Good or bad, things were going to change. She could feel it in the air.

CHAPTER THREE

Cam woke to a pounding headache and a bunch of bad memories. It didn't help to open his bleary eyes and find the view the same as it had been when he was in high school. That made him want to close the world out and go back to sleep again. Maybe he would wake up in a better place.

No such luck. He opened his eyes again a few minutes later and nothing had changed. He was still a wimp for having let himself be talked into coming back here. Still an unfit driver for having crashed his car just because of a freak tire blowout. Still an idiot for having had too much to drink and letting it show.

And still bummed at finding Diana more appealing than ever and at the same time, totally unavailable. Life wasn't exactly glowing with happy discovery for him right now.

Then there had been the humiliating way he'd returned to the green green grass of home. His mother had tried to pretend he was fine and gave him the usual hugs and kisses a mother would bestow upon a return-

ing miscreant. But, his father barely acknowledged his
return. And Janey was plotting ways to undermine him
and making no bones about it. He groaned. The outlook
wasn't bright.

There was one more gauntlet to brave—the most important one right now—his grandfather. There was no
point in putting it off any longer.

He made the water in his shower as cold and
stinging as he could stand. He needed to wash away the
previous day and start over. Maybe if he could just
start fresh…

But he already knew it was going to take all his will
to be able to stay and do what he'd promised he would
do—save the family business, and in so doing, hopefully, save the family.

Funny that it would be up to him. When he'd left ten
years before, his grandfather had just disowned him and
his father had refused to take his side. His mother was
upset about his choice of friends, and his sister was
angling to take over his position in the family. To some
extent, a somewhat typical twenty-one-year-old experience. But it had all been a culmination of years of un-
happiness and bad relations, and something had snapped
inside him. He'd had enough. He was going and he was
never coming back.

Leaving Diana behind had been the only hard part.
At eighteen, she'd still been gawky, a coltlike girl whose
antics made him laugh with quick affection. She thought
she needed him, though he knew very well she was
strong enough to handle things on her own. She was fun

and interesting and she was also the only person who seemed to understand what he was talking about most of the time.

But that was then. Things were different now. Diana had proven she could make it on her own, no problem. She'd done just fine without him. And she now belonged to somebody else. She could deny it, but the facts were right there, front and center. She was pregnant. That meant there was a man in her life. Even if he was out of the picture for the moment, he was there. How could it be any other way?

And all that was just as well, actually. Without that complication, he knew he could have easily fallen in love with her. He'd known that from the moment he saw her coming down to the lake, looking like an angel. He responded to her in a way he never did with other women, a combination of past experiences and current attraction. Yes, he could fall hard. And falling in love was something he was determined never to do again.

For just a moment he thought about Gina, the woman he'd lived with for two years and had almost married. But thoughts of Gina only brought pain, so he shrugged them away.

He needed to focus on the purpose of his return. He needed to get ready to face his grandfather.

Diana parked in the same spot she'd used earlier that morning. This time there was a buzz of activity all around the compound. Workmen were putting new doors on the multiple garages and a painter was freshening up the long white fence that edged the driveway. Across the patio, two men were digging postholes for what looked to be a new barbecue center. With all this action, she could see she wasn't going to need to contemplate a break-in this time. Sighing with satisfaction, she slid out of the car and made her way to the back entrance.

She'd traded in her nightgown for a sleek pantsuit she'd picked up in Carmel a few months before. Luckily she could still fit into it. She'd chosen it out of her closet specifically to rival anything Janey might be wearing. It had a high collar and a loose jacket that hid her belly and she knew she looked pretty good in it—always a confidence booster.

The back door was propped open and she went on into the huge kitchen, where Rosa, elbow deep in flour, waved at her from across the room.

"Mrs. Van Kirk is out in the rose garden," she called. "She asked that you meet her out there to go over some new plans."

"Fine." She waved back at the cheery woman and headed into the house. She'd been here often enough lately to know her way around. This place that had seemed so special to her as a child, and then so scary when she was friends with Cam but never invited in, was now a part of her workspace.

Walking down the long hall, gleaming with Brazilian cherry hardwood, she glanced into the library, and then the parlor, to check on the large arrangements she'd brought just a few days before. Both looked pretty good.

Ever since she'd stressed to Rosa that the stems could use a trim and fresh water every few days, her masterpieces were holding up better than they had before.

The Van Kirk mansion was beautiful in a way few houses could be. The quality of the original materials and workmanship shone through. The rich past and full history just added luster. It made her happy and proud just to be here, walking its beautiful halls.

As she rounded the stairwell to head into the dining room and out the French doors, Cam surprised her by arriving down the stairs and stopping right in front of her.

"Good morning, Miss Collins," he said smoothly. "You're back."

She cocked her head to the side and looked him over, fighting hard to suppress her reaction as her heart began a frantic dance in her chest. Here he was. It was really true. She hadn't dreamed what had happened the night before. Cam was back in her life, just when she'd thought it could never be.

He looked so good. Morning sunlight was even more flattering to his handsome face than starlight had been. Dressed in khakis and a blue polo shirt that matched his eyes, he looked hard and muscular as an athlete but gentle as a lover at the same time.

The perfect man—hadn't that always been the problem? She'd never found anyone better. It made her half-angry, half-thrilled, and practically hopeless. Now that he was back, what was going to happen to her peace of mind?

One casual meeting and she was already straying into

thoughts she'd vowed to stay away from. A simple look into that silver-blue gaze and her breath was harder to find and she was thinking moonlight and satin sheets and violins on the terrace. Given half a chance, she would be sliding into his arms, raising her lips for kisses….

No! She couldn't let that happen.

Very quickly, so quickly she hoped he didn't even notice, she pulled herself up short and forced a refocus. Cam was a friend and that was all he could ever be.

So think friend, she ordered herself. Lover thoughts are not allowed.

"Yes," she agreed, putting steel in her spine. "I'm… I'm back."

His gaze swept over her. "You're looking particularly lovely today," he noted, a slight smile softening the corners of his wide mouth.

The corners of her own mouth quirked. "As opposed to what I looked like yesterday, after midnight?" she said, half teasing.

His grin was crooked. "Oh, no. After midnight you looked even better. Only…"

"Did you see a doctor last night?" she broke in quickly, eager to forestall any flirting he might have in mind. They had to keep their relationship on a certain level and she was bound and determined she would be the watchdog of that if he wouldn't be.

"I guess so." He shrugged. "I was pretty much out of it."

"Yes, you were."

Looking chagrined, he put his hand over his heart and

gazed earnestly into her eyes. "I don't drink, you know. Not really. Hardly ever."

If she wasn't careful, he was going to make her laugh, and that was almost as dangerous as making her swoon.

"So you said."

"And it's true. If I'd found a box of crackers in the trunk of the car instead of a bottle of booze, I'd have been all crumbs last night, instead of the sauced serenader I devolved into."

She choked and his eyes sparkled with amusement at his own joke.

"But I do want to apologize. I was rude last night. I took over your lake and ruined your sleep and generally made myself into a damned nuisance."

He meant it. He was really apologizing. She met his gaze in solemn candor. "You did."

"And I'm sorry." His blue eyes were filled with tragic regret.

She laughed softly, shaking her head. She'd missed him, missed his candor, missed his teasing and missed what often actually seemed to be his sincere sensitivity to what she was feeling. But she had to admit, that sensitivity could sometimes slosh over into a subtle mockery and she was afraid he might be working his way in that general direction right now.

Still, they were friends, weren't they? She was allowed to act like a friend, at least.

"I'm not," she said firmly. "I'm not a bit sorry." She smiled up into his face. "Despite everything, it is good to have you back in the neighborhood."

"'Despite everything,' you say." He looked skeptical. "Seriously?"

Her smile deepened. "Of course."

The warmth between them began to sizzle and she knew it was time to pull back. But it felt like resisting quicksand to do it. If only she could allow herself this small island of pleasure. Soon enough she would leave and hopefully wall off any further contact with Cam, except the most casual and occasional kind. Would it really ruin everything to let herself enjoy him, just for this warm spring morning?

Yes. He was looking at her mouth and it sent shivers all through her. She couldn't risk even a tiny moment or two of weakness. Determined, she pulled away.

"I drove by to look at your car this morning," she said over her shoulder as she started to walk toward the French doors that opened onto the gardens.

"How's it doing?" he asked, walking with her.

She glanced at him sideways. "You didn't tell me you'd had a tire blow out."

"Didn't I?"

"No." She stopped in the doorway, turning to face him again. "It's too bad. I sort of liked your story about fighting the wheel in order to get to my place."

He snapped his fingers. "That was exactly what I was doing when the blowout occurred."

She grinned. "Right."

Mrs. Van Kirk, wearing a wide-brimmed sun hat and carrying a basket filled with cut flowers, was out among her prized rosebushes and as she turned, she spotted the two of them and began to wave. "Yoo-hoo! My dear, I'm over here."

Diana lifted her hand to wave back and said out of the corner of her mouth, "Who's she talking to, you or me?"

He stood beside her in the doorway, looking out. "I'd say it's a toss-up."

She glanced at him. "She's your mother."

His eyes narrowed suspiciously as he looked out at where she stood, waving at them. "Sometimes I wonder," he muttered.

Diana didn't wonder. In fact, she didn't have a doubt. Cam looked so much like his mother, it was cute—or frightening, depending on how you looked at it.

"Well, I'm going to go to her," Diana said, turning to leave.

He hung back. "I'm not coming with you. I've got a command audience with my grandfather."

"Oh, no." Stopping, she looked back at him. "Is this the first you've seen him since you came back?"

He nodded, a faraway look in his eyes. "This should be interesting."

To say the least. Diana winced, remembering all those old, painful arguments with the old man when he was younger. She could see by the look on his face that he wasn't as optimistic about the coming meeting as he might pretend.

"I'm surprised you're not taking in a bodyguard," she said lightly, only half joking. "I remember those sessions you used to have with him." Her eyes widened as she recalled some especially wild fights they'd had and she shuddered. "He put you through the wringer."

Cam nodded and he didn't smile. "That he did." His gaze skimmed over her face. "You want to come with me?"

She reared back. "Not on your life. When I was suggesting a bodyguard, I was thinking more along the lines of one of those burly fellows digging posts for the new barbecue center out back."

He laughed. "I think I can handle my grandfather," he said. "I'm older now. Wiser." He cocked an eyebrow. "More agile."

Diana shook her head, suppressing a grin. "And besides," she reminded him. "From what I hear, he's often bedridden. I guess that would give you an advantage."

He laughed again. "Exactly."

Word was that his grandfather was in rapidly failing health. With Cam's father spending most of his time at spa resorts that specialized in "rest cures" and his sister reportedly caught up in playing musical husbands, that left Cam to support his mother and help make some decisions. She was beginning to realize that those circumstances were probably part of the reason he'd agreed to come back home.

"I'll come out and join you if I survive."

"Okay." She winced as she started out through the rosebushes. She shouldn't be encouraging any of this "joining" or chatting or anything else with Cam. Her goal coming in had been to have the meeting with Mrs. Van Kirk and then get out of here as quickly as possible.

It was becoming more and more clear that staying away from Cam had to be her first priority.

The older woman came toward her, smiling.

"Oh, my dear, I'm so glad to see you. Thank you so much for coming by. Come sit with me in the garden and Rosa will bring us some nice tea."

Diana smiled back and followed her to the little gazebo at the far side of the flower garden. Her relationship with Cam's mother had undergone a complete transformation in the last few years. When she was a teenager, she knew very well the woman had considered her a guttersnipe who would contaminate her son if she didn't keep a constant vigil. The one time Cam had tried to bring her into the house, Mrs. Van Kirk had practically barred the door with her own plump body.

Years later, after Cam was long gone and Diana had started her flower business, the woman had hired her periodically, acting rather suspicious at first, but warming to her little by little as the quality of her work became apparent. By now, her affection for the girl she used to scorn was amazingly obvious to everyone—and sometimes resented by Janey.

But Diana was comfortable meeting with her, and she settled into a chair across from her in the gazebo, thinking once again how similar some of her features were to Cam's. She'd been a beautiful woman and was still very attractive in a plush sort of way. Her hair was auburn where Cam's was almost black, and her look was soft rather than hard, but she had the same blue eyes and sweet smile he did.

"I want to tell you how much I appreciate you bringing my son home last night after that terrible accident," Mrs. Van Kirk began. "He was certainly out of sorts for a while, but Dr. Timmer assures us there will be no lasting injuries. He was so fortunate it happened so close to your place." Her gaze sharpened and she frowned. "How exactly did you know the accident had happened?"

"Just lucky I guess," Diana said breezily. This was not the time to go into reasons why Cam felt at home enough on her property to use it as a refuge. "I was glad to be able to help."

"Yes," she said, gazing at Diana as though seeing her with new eyes. "Well, anyway, we'll have tea." She signaled toward the kitchen, where Rosa had appeared at the door. The housekeeper waved that she understood, and Mrs. Van Kirk turned back to the subject at hand.

"Now, I want you to take a look at my new roses." She pointed out a pair of new English heirlooms. "What do you think of them?"

"Oh, they're lovely. That soft violet color is just brilliant."

She looked pleased. "Yes, I've hired a new rose expert to come in twice a week and advise me. I want to make sure I'm getting the right nutrients to my little babies. He's very expensive but I'm so pleased with his work." She looked up. "Perhaps you know him. Andre Degregor?"

Diana nodded. "Yes, he's quite good." And an internationally recognized rose expert. "Expensive" was probably putting it mildly.

"You seem to be doing a lot of work on the estate," she noted, giving the older woman an opening to get the conversation back on track.

"Yes." She settled down in her seat and gave Diana a significant smile. "And that's why I wanted to see you. I'm going to begin a major project. And I want you to take a primary role in the preparations."

"A project?" she echoed brightly. What type of project would involve a flower stylist? She was beginning to feel a faint thread of trepidation about this. "What sort of project?"

"It's something I've been thinking about for a long time." Her eyes were shining with excitement. "I'm planning a whole series of various social gatherings—teas, dinner parties, barbecues, card parties—all culminating in a major ball at the end of next month."

"Oh my," Diana said faintly.

"On top of that, we'll be hosting quite a few guests between functions. I've hired a wonderful caterer from San Francisco—for the whole month!" She laughed with delight at the thought. "And I want to hire you for the decorating. If all goes as planned, this will be quite an undertaking."

"It certainly sounds like it."

"Now, I'm going to want you to put some extra effort into your weekly arrangements and prepare to work up an entire decorating plan for the various parties."

"Really." Diana's smile felt stiff and artificial as she began to mull over the implications. She had a very bad feeling about this. Ordinarily she would be welcoming the new business, but something told her she wasn't going to like this once she got the full picture.

Rosa arrived with a tray containing a sterling silver teapot and two lovely, egg-shell thin porcelain cups with saucers, along with a plate of crisp, slender cookies. Out of the corner of her eye, Diana could see Janey making her way into the garden and she offered up a fervent prayer that the young woman would find her way out again before stopping in to see them. She had enough to deal with here without Janey's caustic comments.

"You have such a good eye for decorating, Diana. I'm really going to be counting on you to help make this very special."

"What is the theme going to be?" she asked as Rosa poured the tea.

"Well, what could be more obvious?" She waved a hand dramatically and leaned forward. "I'm planning to introduce Cam back into the society he should have been a part of all these years," she said emphatically. "That's the theme."

"The theme," Janey said, flouncing into the gazebo and flopping down into a wicker chair, "is that Mother wants to marry Cam off to the most important socialite she can find for him, and preferably the one with the most money. He's raw meat for the voracious upper crust marriage market."

Her words stung, but Diana kept smiling. After all, she'd known this was coming, hadn't she? Cam had said as much, though he'd tried to take it back. He'd come back home to get married.

"Janey!" Mrs. Van Kirk said sharply.

Her daughter shrugged. "It's true, Mother, and you know it. We need the money."

The woman's sense of decorum was being challenged by her daughter's gloomy vision of reality and she didn't like it at all.

"Janey, I will thank you to keep your acid tongue to yourself. We have no financial problems. We've always been able to live just the way we've wanted to live. We're going to be just fine."

"Dream on, Mom." Janey looked at Diana and shrugged. "She won't look out and see the tsunami coming. But you might as well know it's on its way."

The older woman pretended not to hear. "Now, I want you to think this over, Diana. I'm hoping you'll be free." She sighed happily. "Such a lot of activity! It will be just like the old days."

"What old days are those, Mother?" Janey asked, the tiniest hint of sarcasm edging her tone.

"Oh, I don't know." Her mother frowned at her. "Things were more hectic when you children were younger. We had parties. Remember all those picnics we had when you were sixteen? It's been a long time since we've had an actual event here. It's exciting, don't you think?"

Diana was torn. On the one hand, she liked Cam's mother, despite her eccentricities—or maybe because of them. On the other hand, she didn't want to be involved in roping Cam into a marriage—any marriage, good or not. The very thought was darn depressing. It would be awful to see him make a bad marriage just for his mother's sake, but it would be almost worse to see him falling in love with some beautiful young debutante.

Either way, Diana would be the loser.

But that was crazy and she knew it. Cam would marry someone. He had to. It was only natural. She only wished he would do it far away where she didn't have to know about it.

"Poor Cam is going to be sold off to the highest bidder," Janey said. "I wish him better luck in marriage than I've had. But then, I tend to marry penniless jerks, so there you go."

"Janey, please," Mrs. Van Kirk said icily. She'd had enough. "I'd like to talk to Diana alone. We need to plan."

For a moment, Diana thought Janey was going to refuse to leave, but she finally rolled her eyes and rose with a look of disdain on her face. Diana watched her go and for once, she wished she could go along.

How was she going to tell Cam's mother that she couldn't do this? She hated to disappoint her, especially when she was so excited about her project. But the situation was downright impossible. She was going to have to find the right words…somehow.

And in the meantime, she was going to have to find a way to keep Cam at a distance.

CHAPTER FOUR

FILLED with comforting tea and discomforting misgivings, Diana skirted the house as she made her way back toward her car, hoping to avoid seeing Cam.

No such luck. He came around a corner of the house and met her under the vine-covered pergola.

"Hey," he said, looking surprised.

"Hay is for horses," she said back tersely, giving him barely a glance and trying to pass him.

"Channeling our school days, are we?" He managed to fill the passageway, giving her no room to flee. "I guess the meeting didn't go so well."

She looked up at him and sighed. "Oh, it went fine. I'm just a little jumpy today." She made a show of looking at her watch. "I've really got to go. I'm late."

He didn't buy it. Folding his arms across his chest, he cocked his head to the side and regarded her narrowly. "Late for what?"

She hesitated, not ready to make something up on the fly. "None of your business," she said instead. "I just need to go."

He stepped forward, suddenly looking concerned, glancing down at her slightly protruding belly. "Are you okay? Do you need help?"

He was being too darn nice. Her eyes stung. If he kept this up, she might end up crying, and that would be a disaster. Shaking her head, she sighed again and decided she might as well tell him the truth. Lifting her chin resolutely, she forced herself to meet his gaze.

"I'm going to be perfectly honest, Cam. I…I need to keep my distance from you. With all these plans and all that's going on, I can't spend time with you. It just won't work."

He looked completely baffled. "What are you talking about?"

She took a deep breath and plunged in. "Your mother just spent an hour telling me all about the plans to find you a wife. She wants me to help." She took a deep breath, praying her voice wouldn't break. "I don't think I can be involved in that."

"Diana, it's not a problem." His laugh was short and humorless. "She can look all she wants. I'm not getting married."

She blinked up at him, not sure why he would say such a thing. "But you said last night…"

He gave her his famously crooked grin. "I think I said a lot of crazy things last night. Don't hold me to any of them."

"Cam…"

"I'll tell you one thing." He grimaced and raked his fingers through his dark hair, making it stand on end in a way she found eminently endearing. "I'm never going to drink alcohol again."

"Good. You'll live longer and be healthier." She shook her head. She wasn't really worried about that. "Why did you say you'd come back to get married if you don't mean to do it? Maybe the alcohol brought out your true feelings."

He groaned. "What are you now, a psychologist in your spare time? Forget it. This is a 'don't try this at home' situation." He shook his head, looking at her earnestly. "Diana, my mother has been trying to get me to come home and get married for years. I've resisted. I'm still resisting. But she's still trying. That's all there is to it."

She frowned suspiciously. "Okay, you're saying you didn't come home to get married?"

"Of course not."

She waved a hand in the air. "But then why is your mother planning all this?"

"She's always planning things. That's how she lives her life." He shrugged. "Let her go on planning. It'll keep her busy and out of the way."

She frowned, not sure she could accept that. "I don't know."

Reaching out, he took hold of her shoulders, fingers curling around her upper arms, and stared down into her face. "Okay, Diana, here's the honest truth. My mother can make all kinds of plans, for all kinds of parties. She can even plan a wedding if she wants to. But I'm not marrying anybody." His added emphatically, "Anybody. Ever."

Anybody...ever...

The words echoed in her head but it was hard to think straight with his warm hands holding her and his hard body so close. A breeze tumbled through the yard and a cloud of pink bougainvillea blossoms showered down around them. She looked up into his starry blue eyes and had to resist getting lost there.

"What happened to you, Cam?" She heard the words as though from far away and it took a moment to realize the voice was her own.

He hesitated, staring down into her eyes as though he didn't want to let her go. The warning signs were there. She had to pull away. And yet, it seemed almost impossible. When her body wouldn't react, she had only her voice to reach for as a defensive weapon.

"Cam, what is it? What do you have against marriage?"

Her words seemed to startle him and his head went back. He stared at her for a few seconds, then grimaced.

"Once bitten, twice shy," he muttered, releasing her and making a half turn away from where she stood, shoving his hands down into his pockets.

Watching him, shock shot through her system and she barely avoided gasping. What was he saying? Did he really mean what it seemed he meant?

"You've been married?" she said, coming down to earth with a thump.

"No," he responded, looking back at her, his eyes hard. "But I did come close. Not a pretty story, and I'm not about to tell it. Just understand I've been inoculated. I've stared into the abyss and I've learned from that. I won't need another warning."

She didn't know why she was so disturbed by what he was saying. He was a normal man, after all. No, strike that, he was an abnormally attractive man, but with a normal man's needs and desires. Of course he'd had women in his life these last ten years. Naturally he'd been in love. What could be more ordinary? Just because *she* was a nut case and couldn't forget Cam for long enough to have a relationship with another man didn't have any bearing on his experiences. Some amateur psychologist she was; she couldn't even fix her own life, much less dabble in his.

"Well, if that's true, you'd better tell your mother," she said, grasping at the remnants of their conversation to steady herself on. "It's not fair to let her give parties and invite people."

"I said we should let her make plans. I never said she could put on any parties."

She shook her head. "That doesn't make a lot of sense."

"Don't you think I know that?"

He looked so troubled, she wanted to reach out and comfort him. If only she had the right to do it. But then she remembered—even if she had that right, she would have had to stop herself. She couldn't risk doing anything that might draw them closer. She had to think of her child.

"I've got to go," she said, turning and starting toward where her car was parked.

"I'll walk you out to your car," he said, coming along with her.

She walked quickly, hoping to stay at least an arm's length from him. She just had to get away.

"Diana's Floral Creations," he said aloud, reading the sign painted in pretty calligraphy on the side of her tiny little van. "Interesting name."

She threw him a look over her shoulder. "It's pretty generic, I know. I'm creative with flowers, not with words."

"No, I meant it. I like it. It suits you."

She hesitated, wanting to get into her car and go, but at the same time, not wanting to leave him.

"What made you go into this flower business stuff?" he asked her, actually seeming interested.

She smiled. This was a subject she loved. She was on firmer footing here. "I've always been good with plants. And I needed something to do on my own. I took horticulture classes in college so I had some background in it. Then I worked in a flower shop part-time for a couple of years."

He nodded, his gaze skimming over her and his admiration for her obvious. That gave her the impetuous to go on, tell him more.

"It's really a wonderful line of work. Flowers are so special, and used for such special occasions. We use them to celebrate a birthday, or a baby being born or two people getting married—or even the life of someone who has died. They add something to the most emotional times of our lives. And that interests and excites me."

"And also just to decorate a room," he reminded her, since that was what she was doing here at his house.

"Yes," she agreed. "But usually flowers are used to represent an emotion. They're symbols of feelings people have a hard time expressing in words." She stopped, coloring a bit, not used to being so effusive about her line of work. For some reason, she'd felt the need to tell him, explain. Well, now she had. She turned to her car, ready to make her escape.

But he stopped her once again.

"I'm glad you have something you love so much," he told her. "The business I've been running is a bit more prosaic." He hesitated, then grimaced.

"Okay, Di," he said, looking down at her. "I might as well get this off my chest. Here it is. The real reason I came home, the reason behind everything I'm going to be doing for the foreseeable future."

She waited, heart beating, wondering if she really wanted to hear this. She knew instinctively that whatever it was he was about to reveal would have the effect of tying her more closely to this family—this crazy outlandish bunch of people who had once scorned her and her family. And now he was going to tell her something that would make her care about them. It didn't seem altogether fair. But then, life wasn't often fair, was it?

He turned from her, flexed his shoulders and then turned back.

"There won't be any parties. There can't be any parties. The fact is, there's no money."

Diana heard what he said, but she couldn't quite digest it. Janey had said things that had let her know money was probably a consideration, even a concern, but to say there wasn't any... That just seemed crazy.

These were the Van Kirks. They had always been the richest family in town.

"What? What are you saying?"

"I've just been talking to Grandfather, finding out how bad it is. He already outlined the situation to me over the phone a few weeks ago. That's why I came home. And now I know the rest of the story." He took a deep breath and a pained expression flashed across his face. "My family is on the verge of losing everything."

Her head came up. Despite the things his sister had said, she would never have dreamed it could come to this. "You mean bankruptcy?"

He nodded. "I came home for one reason, Di. I came home to try to save my parents from losing their home."

"Oh, Cam, no."

He went on, detailing where the problems lay and how long they had festered, but Diana was thinking about his mother and remembering how she'd seemed oblivious to the dangers as Janey had taunted her with them. She'd thought Cam's sister was exaggerating, but it seemed she was wrong.

She knew without having him explain it that the issue went back years and years. Many of those old fights Cam had with his grandfather centered around the old man's fear that Cam would end up being a drone like his father was. She'd been vaguely aware at the time that Cam's dad had tried running the family affairs and had failed miserably, mostly through his own weaknesses. The grandfather had been trying to groom Cam to be a better manager. Even though Cam hadn't stayed here to take his father's place, it seemed he'd found his way in the world and made something of himself. And now it was Cam whom the grandfather had turned to in hopes of getting the family out of this mess. She wondered if he really had the experience. She knew he had the family background for it. And with his grandfather as his mentor, surely there would be hope that he could use his younger energy to turn things around.

No wonder Cam had been called back. Someone had to rescue the family, she supposed. Why he'd decided to let them pull him back, after all he'd said when he left, was another question, one she couldn't answer.

But there was no doubt the situation was dire. Bankruptcy sounded so radical. And the Van Kirks not living in the Van Kirk mansion? Unthinkable.

Still, this couldn't be her problem. She couldn't let it be. The more Cam talked, the more she wanted to go to him, to throw herself into his arms, to tell him she would help in any way she could. But she couldn't do that. She had to get out of this situation. Her baby had to be the main focus of her life, the reason for living. She couldn't get distracted by old longings. She had to get out of here and leave temptation behind. And that meant leaving Cam behind.

"I'm sorry all this is happening," she told him, trying to be firm. "But I really can't be involved. Do you understand?" She gazed up at him earnestly.

He nodded slowly. "Sure. Of course. You have your baby to think of. You need a calm environment. Don't worry about Mother. I'll explain things to her."

A few minutes later, she was in her car and heading for home again, only this time she wasn't crying. Her face was set with determination. She was going to be strong if it killed her.

Diana was up a tree—quite literally—a black oak to be exact. It wasn't something she usually did and that was probably why she seemed to be so bad at it. It was a typical well-meaning rescue mission gone awry.

She been jolted awake early that morning by small, piercing cries from outside. When she'd wrapped herself in a blanket and stepped out to find what tiny creature was in distress, she'd been led, step by step, to the big old black oak. Looking up, she saw the cutest little black kitten staring down at her with huge golden eyes.

"Oh, no, you don't," she'd grumbled at the time, turning back toward the house. "I know very well you'll have an easier time getting down from there than I would in going up. You can do it. You just have to try." She glanced over her shoulder at the little one as she returned to the house. "And then I hope you'll go back wherever you came from."

That had been hours earlier. In the meantime she'd made herself breakfast, taken the time to do a bit of book-keeping for her business and returned some phone calls, including one from her attorney cousin Ben Lanker in Sacramento. It seemed their uncle Luke, the last survivor from the older generation, had died a week before and left a piece of property in the mountains to the two of them, jointly, as the only remaining descendants in their family. She'd received something in the mail that she hadn't understood, but Ben explained what was going on and suggested they get together and talk it over.

She was tempted to put him off. She already had the only piece of land she'd ever wanted and from what Ben said, the inheritance from Uncle Luke might turn out to be more trouble than it was worth.

But then she remembered that she'd been suspicious of her cousin in the past and she decided maybe she'd better look into the facts.

"One shouldn't look an inheritance in the mouth, I suppose," she muttered to herself.

It could just be that Ben was trying to pull a fast one. He had that slippery lawyer way about him. So she told him she would get back to him soon and find a time when they could get together and go over the situation to see what would be best.

In the meantime, the little cries had grown more pitiful with time, wearing away at her like water torture. When storm clouds began to threaten, she finally decided she had to bite the bullet and climb up or she wouldn't be able to live with herself when the worst happened. She kept picturing the exhausted kitten losing all strength and falling to its death through the gnarled branches.

"I'm coming," she said reassuringly as she hoisted herself up with a foothold on the first major branch, regretting that she didn't have any ladders tall enough to do this job. "Just hold on."

It had been a while, but she'd climbed this very tree often when she was young. The only problem was, she wasn't all that young anymore. Muscles and instincts she'd had at that age—not to mention the fearlessness—seemed to be gone. And the tree was a lot bigger. And she was pregnant. To her surprise, that threw her balance off in ways she hadn't expected. But she kept climbing, reaching for the kitten. And every time her fingers almost touched it, the silly little bugger backed away and climbed higher.

"This is not going to work," she said aloud, staring up at the infuriating cat. "I'm not going any farther. You're going to have to come to me."

Fat chance. The golden eyes just got bigger and the cries just got more pathetic.

"Oh, never mind," Diana said, turning away and giving up. And then she looked down.

Somehow, she'd come further than she'd thought. The ground looked very far away. And as she clung to a space between a branch and the trunk, she began to realize she was going to have a heck of a time getting down.

And the kitten was still crying.

"You little brat," Diana muttered to herself. "Look what you've done. You've got me up a tree. How am I going to get down?"

"Meow," the kitten chirped.

And the rain began.

"I can't believe this," she moaned as drops began to spatter all around her. "Why is everything going wrong at once?"

And that was when she heard Cam's car arrive.

"Oh, no!"

She hadn't seen him for the last two days. She'd almost begun to think he might have taken her last words to heart and might just let her be alone, not try to pull her into his life again. But here he was, so she supposed that had been a bad guess.

She sat very still and watched as he turned off the engine and slipped out of the car. He looked around at the trees and the lake, but his gaze didn't rise high enough to notice her and she kept quiet while he went to the front door and knocked. The rain was still light, but it was beginning to make rivulets down her neck.

"Diana?" he called. "You home?"

Now it was time to make a decision. What was she going to do—let him know she was stuck in a tree? Or just sit here and let him drive away again and try to figure out how she was going to get down on her own in a rainstorm?

It was a rather big decision. She felt like a fool sitting here. And yet, she was liable to break her neck if she tried to get down by herself. It was pretty obvious what her decision was going to have to be, but she put it off as long as possible. She couldn't even imagine the humiliation she was going to feel when she began to call out to him, pitiful as the little animal scrabbling around on the branch above her.

Luckily she didn't have to do that. He heard the kitten screeching and finally looked up into the tree on his own. She looked down. He looked up. He fought hard to hold back a big old grin that threatened to take over his handsome face. She tried hard not to stick her tongue out at him. They both failed.

He came over and stood right under where she was. "Good view of the valley from up there?" he asked.

"The best," she answered, her nose in the air. "I come up here all the time."

"Do you?" He bit back a short laugh. "I see you have your faithful feline companion with you. What's the kitty's name?"

"Once you name them, you own them," she warned. For some unknown reason, she was unable to keep the annoyance from her tone. "Do you need a kitten? I'm putting this one up for adoption." She tried to move a bit without losing her footing. "The only catch is, you have to climb up here and get her."

"Well, I don't need a cat," he admitted. "At least not today. But I will help you down."

"I don't need any help," she said quickly, then bit her lower lip. What was she saying?

"You can get down by yourself?" He just couldn't hold the grin back and that was infuriating.

"Of course."

He shrugged. "Okay then. I'll just leave you to your own devices." He turned as though to head for his car.

"Cam! Come back here." She shivered. She was really getting wet. "Of course I need help getting down. Why do you think I'm sitting here like a lump of coal?"

He tried to control the chuckle that was fighting its way out. "A little humility is a wonderful thing," he noted.

She glared at him, but followed his instructions and

a moment later, she took the last leap of faith and ended up in his arms. He held her for a moment, her feet just off the ground, and looked down into her wet face.

"Why is it that every time I see you I want to smile?" he asked.

She tried to glare at him. "You're probably laughing at me."

"No." He shook his head, and his eyes darkened as he looked at her lips. "That's not it."

She drew her breath in and pulled away, regaining her footing and turning toward her little house. "Let's get out of this rain," she said, and as if on cue, it began to pour. They'd barely made the porch when she remembered something.

"Oh, wait! We forgot the kitten!"

"No problem," he said, pointing just behind her.

She whirled. There it was, looking like a drowned rat and staring up at her with those big golden eyes. Despite everything, she laughed. "You little faker! I knew you could get down if you tried."

"I guess you could call this a mission accomplished," Cam said as he opened the door and they all rushed into the warmth of the little house.

"I'll get towels," she said, reaching into her tiny bathroom. "We'd better dry off kitty first. She's liable to catch pneumonia, poor little thing."

Her gaze flickered over Cam as she spoke and she couldn't help but notice the rain had plastered his shirt nicely against the spectacular muscles of his wonderful chest. Why that should give her a sinking feeling in the pit of her stomach she couldn't imagine, and she looked away quickly.

"Here," she said, handing him a towel. "You take this one."

She caught the kitten as it tried to make a dash for the underside of her couch, toweled it down and then let it go. It quickly scampered into the next room.

"I ought to put her out so she can find her way home," she said, shaking her head. "But how can I put her out in the rain?"

"I think you just got yourself a cat," Cam noted, slinging the towel around his neck after rubbing his thick hair with it. "Here. You need a little drying off yourself."

She opened her mouth to protest, but he was already applying a fluffy fresh towel to her wild hair.

"I can do it," she said, reaching for the towel.

"Hold still," he ordered, not letting it go.

She gave in, lifting her face and closing her eyes as he carefully dabbed at the raindrops on her nose. He smiled, remembering the time he'd had to clean her up in similar fashion after a messy exploding bubble gum incident. She'd had more freckles then, but otherwise she looked very much the same.

Then she opened her eyes and the memory of Diana as a young girl faded. She was anything but a young girl now. She was a warm-blooded angel just as he'd seen her the other night. As he gazed down into her dark eyes, he had the sense that his larger vision was picking up details so sharp, so clear, that he could see everything about her—the tiny curls at her hairline, the long, full sweep of her eyelashes, the translucent shimmer of her skin, the clear outline of her beautiful lips. She was a woman—a beautiful, desirable woman, a woman he had known most of his life and loved just as long—loved as a friend, but the affection was very strong just the same.

And yet this was different. This was something more. A jolt of arousal went through him and he drew back quickly, as though he'd touched a live wire. But he didn't turn away. He stood where he was, watching her as she reached for the fluffy towel and began to rub her hair with it.

He knew he'd had indications of this sort of response to her ever since he'd come back, but this time it was so strong, he couldn't pretend to himself that it was anything but exactly what it was. That presented a bit of a problem, a bit of a conflict. He considered her his best friend, but the way he was feeling today was light years beyond friendship. Did he have a right to feel this way? Or was this a big mistake?

She dropped the towel onto the couch and looked at him, a challenge in her dark eyes, as though she had a sense of what he was feeling and wanted to warn him off. He felt clumsy and that wasn't like him. He just wasn't sure…

"Why did you come here today?" she asked him.

He raised one eyebrow, startled at her question. "I wanted to see how you're doing."

"I'm doing fine." She said it crisply, as though that ought to take care of the matter, and he might as well be going.

But that only put his back up and meant he was going to be staying all the longer.

"Actually I haven't been around for the last few days," he went on, "I was down in L.A. talking to some money people, bankers I've got contacts with, trying to work out some sort of deal to stay afloat, at least for now."

The challenge faded from her gaze and a look of concern began to take its place. That reassured him. The Diana he knew was still in there somewhere.

"Any luck?" she asked.

"Marginal luck." He hesitated, then went on. "I did talk to a real estate broker about selling the house."

"Oh." Her hands went to her mouth and her eyes took on a look of tragedy. "That would flat out kill your mother."

"I know."

"You didn't…?"

"Not yet. I'm hoping to avoid it."

She sighed and nodded. "Have you told her there won't be any parties yet?"

He grimaced uncomfortably and didn't meet her gaze for a moment. "Not totally."

"Cam!"

"It's making her so happy to plan." He looked back at her ruefully. "I hate to burst the bubble on her dream."

"But she's hiring people like Andre Degregor and the caterer from San Francisco. You've got to stop her."

He knew that. He had to do something very soon. But right now all he could think about was how this new electricity he felt between the two of them was working out. Not well, he took it, from the look on her face. She was wary and guarded and wanted him to leave. He rubbed the back of his neck and frowned thoughtfully, about to ask her why. But the kitten was back, looking for attention.

"Oh, kitty, what am I going to do with you?" she said, smiling down at it. "I don't need a kitten. I'm having a baby."

His immediate sense was that she'd said that as a reminder to him, and he took it to heart. He knew she was having a baby. That very fact made the way his feelings toward her were evolving all the more problematic.

"What you do need," he said to her, "living out here on your own, is a dog. Whatever happened to Max?"

"Max?" She smiled, thinking of the golden retriever she'd grown up with. "Max died years ago. He was really a great dog, wasn't he?"

Cam nodded, remembering. There was a time when Max had been part of the whole picture, always bounding out to meet him when he came to fish or to see Diana. Realizing he was gone left an empty spot. Nothing lasted forever. Everything changed.

Moving restlessly, he turned and looked around the room.

"You know, I've never been in here before."

She looked surprised, then nodded. "No one was allowed in here while Jed was alive."

His mouth twisted as he remembered. "Your father was something of a barnyard dog around this place, wasn't he?"

"That he was."

He turned back to look at her. She hadn't invited him to sit down. She hadn't offered a drink or something to eat. She wanted him to go, didn't she? He frowned. Funny, but he didn't want to leave. Everything in him rebelled at the thought.

"I came close once," he pointed out. "I came over here full of righteous anger and tried to come in to talk to him."

She looked up, curious. "What about?"

"You. I came to tell him to stop using you for a punching bag."

She flushed and shook her head. "I'm sure he agreed immediately, once you explained to him how naughty it was to beat up on your teenage daughter," she said dryly.

"He pulled out his shotgun." Cam grinned, remembering. "I took off like a scalded cat." He glanced down at the kitten, now wrapped around Diana's ankles.

"No offense intended, kitty," he said glibly before raising his gaze to meet Diana's. Their gazes caught and held for a beat too long, and then she pulled away and turned to pick up the kitten and carry it into the kitchen where she put down a tiny dish of milk from the refrigerator.

He watched, thinking about that time he'd come looking for Jed. He'd called the older man out and told him if he hit her again, he'd take her away from here. She'd told him again and again not to do it, that it would only make things worse for her. But when he found her with bruises on her upper arms and a swollen knot below her blackened eye that day, he'd raged with anger. He'd had enough.

"You do it one more time and I'll take her with me," he'd yelled at Jed. "You won't see her again."

"Where do you think you're going to take her?" Jed had jeered back at him. "Won't nobody take her in."

"I'll take her to my house. We'll take care of her."

Jed had laughed in his face. "You can't take her to your house. Your mother would die before she'd let a little white trash girl like my daughter in on her nice clean floor. Your mother has higher standards, son. You're living in a dream world."

And that was when he'd come out with the shotgun.

Cam had gone home. He told his mother his idea. Funny thing. He'd been so sure his mother would prove Jed wrong. But the man had turned out to have a keener understanding of how things really worked than he did. His mother had been horrified at the idea. She wanted no part of his crazy scheme. Her reaction had been part of what had motivated him to leave home.

Strange how that had changed. Now Diana was one of his mother's favorite people.

She came back out of the little kitchen and looked at him questioningly, as though not really sure why he was still here. But Cam was still lost in the past, mulling over what had happened with her father in the old days.

"When exactly did your dad die?" he asked her.

She told him and he nodded. "Your dad had a grudge against the world and he set about trying to drink himself to death just to spite us all."

She looked troubled and he added, "I suppose your mother dying pretty much threw him for a loop at some point, didn't it?"

Her gaze rose to meet his again. "My mother didn't die. She left when I was six years old."

That sent a shock through him. "I thought she died."

She nodded. Turning from him, she began to collect the towels. "That was what he wanted everyone to think. But the truth was, she couldn't take it anymore and she headed out. Leaving me behind."

Cam felt a wave of sympathy. He could hear the barely concealed heartbreak in her voice. He started to reach for her, but the moment he made a move, he could see her back stiffen, so he dropped his hand back to his side.

"Have you ever heard from her?"

"No." Her chin rose. "And I don't want to."

"I would think you would want to reconnect, especially now with the baby coming."

She whirled, glaring at him. "You know what? My pregnancy is not up for discussion in any way."

"Oh. Okay."

He frowned. His first impulse was to let her set the rules. After all, she was the one who was pregnant. Pregnant women needed extra care, extra tolerance, extra understanding, from what he'd heard. But the more he thought about it, the more he realized he was bending over backward a bit too much. This was getting a little perverse, wasn't it? He turned back and faced her.

"You mean I'm supposed to ignore your baby and pretend it doesn't exist? Is that what you're asking?"

Her face was set as she went on folding the towels and she didn't answer.

Being purposefully defiant, he asked, "So how far along are you, anyway?"

"Cam!" She glared at him, pressing the stack of towels to her chest. "I will not discuss this with you."

He shook his head. "Sorry, Di, that's not going to fly any longer. I need to know what's going on with you and I need to know now."

CHAPTER FIVE

"DIANA, tell me about your baby."

She stared up at him, holding his gaze with her own for a long moment, then she turned and began to march from the room.

He caught up with her, took her by the shoulders and turned her back.

"Come on, Di," he said, carefully being as gentle as he could be, especially in his tone. "You can't run away from it. Tell me."

"Why?" She looked up but her eyes looked more lost than angry. "There's nothing to tell."

He shook his head and his hands caressed her shoulders. "You can't do this. You can't keep it all wrapped up inside you."

She looked almost tearful. "You don't know what you're talking about."

"That's just it. I'm trying. But you've got to let me in."

She shook her head, her hair flying wildly around her face.

"Come on, Diana. We're friends. Remember? We need to stand together."

She looked up, still shaking her head, but slowly. "Cam…"

"It's me, Cam. You can count on me. But you've got to trust me first."

She sighed and he smiled, coaxing her.

"What are you going to name your baby, Di? Have you picked anything out yet? Tell me. Please?"

She swallowed hard and looked away. When you came right down to it, there was no one else in the world she trusted like she trusted Cam. That was just a fact of life and she couldn't deny it.

"I'm going to call her Mia," she said softly. "My mother's name was Mia."

At any other time, Cam would have been horrified to feel his own eyes stinging, but for once, he didn't care. "Oh, Di," he said with all the affection he had at his disposal. "Oh, sweetheart." And he pulled her close against him. "That's a beautiful name."

Her arms came up, and for just a moment, she clung to him. He pressed a kiss into her hair and held her close. And then she pulled away, all stiff again, and took a step back.

"When is Mia due?" he asked, hoping to keep the connection from breaking again.

But she shook her head and looked as though she regretted what she'd already told him.

"What are your plans? How are you doing physically? Diana, what can I do to help you?"

She took another step away from him. "I'm fine," she said shortly. "Just leave it at that, Cam. I'm doing fine."

He shook his head. "Don't lock me out, Diana."

She stared at him for a long moment, then sighed and said, "Don't you see? I have to lock you out. If I don't…"

"What?" He shook his head. He didn't see at all. "What will happen if you don't?"

She swallowed hard, as though this was very difficult, but she held her shoulders high and went on quickly.

"Here's the deal, Cam. You were my savior when I was a kid. You defended me from the bullies. You made life seem worthwhile. I was going through a pretty rough time where it looked like the world was against me. And then you came."

She closed her eyes for a moment, remembering that day. "And suddenly I had a champion. It made a huge difference in my life and I thank you for it to this day. But…"

He sighed. "Oh, yes, I thought I could sense a 'but' coming."

"In some ways you ruined me."

He stared at her, shocked. "Ruined you?"

"This is how. My expectations in what a man should be, in what I wanted in a man to share my life, became unrealistic. You raised the bar so darn high, I couldn't find a man who could clear it."

He looked at her in complete bewilderment and was close to laughing, but he knew that would be the kiss of death.

"That's nuts."

"No, it's true. I'm serious." She shrugged and sighed.

"I don't know if it was the real you or my enhanced imaginary you."

He groaned. "You make me sound like an action figure."

"But that image was hard for any man to overcome." She bit her lip and then went on. "I tried. For years, I tried. But I couldn't get you out of my mind." She hesitated, wanting to leave it at that. Going any further would be getting a bit risky. But she knew there was a bit more that she had to say.

"So I finally took some affirmative steps and moved forward. I had to. And now suddenly, here you are." She shook her head and looked at him as though pleading for his understanding. "I can't let myself slide back to being that dependent little girl I was in the past. I just can't let that happen."

"I understand that," he said, though it was only partly true. "I respect you for it."

She searched his eyes. "But do you understand that I can't be around you? You distort my reality."

He hesitated, wishing he knew how best to deal with this. Bottom line, he didn't want to take himself completely out of her life. He just couldn't imagine that happening. And he still didn't really believe in all this on a certain level. "That can be fixed."

"No, it can't." She took a step back away from him, as though she'd begun to realize he didn't really understand at all. "I have a baby to think about now. She has to be my focus. Cam, I just can't be around you. I can't live my life hoping to see you smile, hoping to have a minute with you, watching as you go on with what you do. Don't you see that?"

She meant it. He could see it in her face. He rubbed his neck and frowned at her. "This is crazy."

"It only seems crazy to you because you haven't thought about it like I have. Believe me, I've lived it for years. I think I have a better grasp of what I have going on inside, in my heart and soul, than you do. I know what I'm talking about." She looked so earnest. "Please, Cam. Don't come here anymore."

Now that was just too much. "What are you talking about?"

"I need you to leave me alone."

He shook his head, still avoiding the implications of her insistence. "So you're telling me…"

"I'm telling you I need space. This is a hard time for me right now and I need space away from you while I learn what I can do, and what I need."

He felt very much at sea. On one hand, he could understand that she might have had some problems. She was raised to have problems. How could she have avoided it? But he didn't see why she was taking it all so seriously. The problems all seemed repairable to him. If he wasn't around, if they were never together, how could these things be fixed? No, her insistence that he stay away didn't seem reasonable.

There was only one explanation he could think of, one factor that might make her so adamant about keeping him out of her life, and she wasn't bringing it up at all. Turning slowly, he asked the pertinent question.

"Is the baby's father liable to show up anytime soon?" he asked.

Something changed in her face. Turning on a dime, she strode to the door and threw it open.

"Go," she said.

And there was just enough anger brewing in him by that time to do exactly what she said without another word.

It was two days later before Diana saw Cam again.

Thursday was her regular day to change the flower arrangements at the Van Kirk mansion. She usually went in the afternoon, but once she found out that Mrs. Van Kirk was going to a garden club lecture at 10:00 a.m., she slipped in early in hopes of missing her. The last thing she wanted was to have the woman try to pin her down on when she would be available to begin work on the "project."

From what Cam had told her, she assumed the project was as good as dead. Though she felt sorry for Cam's mother, that did get her off the hook as far as having to come up with an excuse as to why she couldn't participate. It just wasn't clear when Cam would finally tell his mother the truth. She was going to have to have some sort of conversation about it sooner or later, but hopefully things would be settled down before that came about.

She parked in her usual spot and saw none of the usual family cars. Good. That meant she had the house to herself—except for Rosa, of course. And then there was the grandfather.

She'd never had a conversation with the old man, though she'd seen him out in the gazebo a time or two when she'd come to change the flowers. Funny, for a man who had been such an influence on the valley, and had made such an impression on Cam's life, he was almost invisible these days. As far as she knew, he spent most of his time in his room in a far wing of the house. Even though she would be working in the house for the next hour or so, she didn't expect to run into him.

She replaced the sagging gladiolas in the library with a fresh assortment of spring flowers and moved on into the dining room where she began weeding out lack-luster roses and replacing them with a huge glass bowl holding a mix of yellow tulips and deep purple Dutch irises. At the last minute, she pulled out a few extras and a couple of bud vases and headed for the stairs. She always liked to put a small arrangement in Mrs. Van Kirk's sitting room, and while she was at it, she might as well surprise Cam with a small vase, too. Just because she didn't want to meet him face-to-face didn't mean she wasn't thinking about him.

Thinking about him—hah! She was obsessing on him and she knew it had to stop. But ignoring him when she was handing out flowers wasn't going to fix that problem.

She dropped off one vase in Mrs. Van Kirk's room, then went down the hall to where she thought Cam's room must be. The door was slightly ajar and she knocked softly, then pushed it open enough to confirm her assumption. There was a large bed and a bedside table and cabinets against one wall. Banners and sports items from ten years before filled the other wall. Nobody had made the bed yet and the covers were thrown back casually.

"Naughty Cam," she murmured to herself. What was he waiting for, maid service? He should make his own bed.

She set the small vase with one yellow tulip and one blue iris on the stand beside the bed, then stood back to admire it. Her gaze strayed to the bed itself, and she noted the impression on the pillow where his head had been, then groaned at the way it warmed her just to think of him asleep. She really was a sucker for romance—as long as Cam was the man in the fantasy.

A noise from the hallway turned her head and in that same moment, the door to the attached bathroom opened and Cam came out wearing nothing but a very skimpy towel.

She froze, mouth open, disbelief paralyzing her. In the split second it took to recognize him, he erased the distance between them with one long step, grabbed her and put a hand over her mouth. She gasped as he pulled her tight against him and nudged the door closed with his foot.

"Shh," he whispered against her ear. "Someone's in the hall."

She only struggled for a second or two before she realized that he was just trying to keep her from speaking out loud and making it obvious to whomever was out there that she was in here with a nearly naked Cam. She nodded and then she sagged into his arms and he slipped his hand from her mouth and just held her. The voices went past the room slowly. She thought she recognized Janey's voice, but not the woman with her.

But it hardly mattered. By the time the voices faded, she was lost in a dream. She was in Cam's arms. Hadn't she always imagined it would feel this way? She looked up into Cam's face. His eyes were brimming with laughter, but as she met his gaze, the humor evaporated quickly, as though he could see what she was feeling, and his arms tightened around her.

She had to pull away, she had to stop this, but for some reason, she couldn't. Every muscle she possessed was in rebellion. She felt like she was trying to move in honey—she couldn't do it. Her body, her mind, her soul, all wanted to stay right there and be held by Cam.

His eyes darkened and a sense of something new seemed to throb between them. And then he was bending closer and she gasped just before his mouth covered hers. At that point, she gave up trying. Her own lips parted and her body seemed to melt into his. She accepted him as though she'd been waiting for this all her life.

And she had.

Cam hadn't exactly planned to do this. In fact, he'd been pretty rough on himself, swearing he wouldn't do this or anything like it in rather strong terms. All those things she'd said had been rattling around in his head for the last two days. The more he thought about it the more they didn't make any sense to him—and his own reaction to them made even less sense. He'd always known she had a bit of a crush on him, but he hadn't taken it seriously. That had been long ago—kid's stuff. Things had changed. He'd changed. That was just the point.

So had she changed, too? Were his instincts right? Had her crush turned into something stronger? And if so, what was stopping her from following her instincts and responding to these new currents between them?

The baby's father, of course. What else could it be?

On a certain level, he had to respect that. The bond between a woman and the father of her baby was sacred, even if there were problems between them. He had to stay back, out of the way, and let her deal with the things she needed to deal with.

On the other hand, where the hell was the guy? What kind of a jerk was he? How could he leave Di alone to handle all these life changes on her own? She needed support. She needed her friends around her, if nothing else. As a good friend, how could he ignore that?

But she'd asked him to stay away. Reluctantly he would do the honorable thing and keep his distance, leave her alone.

But, dammit, how could he do that if she showed up in his bedroom like this? *Game over, Diana!*

He had her in his arms and he wanted her there. He had her fresh, sweet scent in his head and the excitement of her touch on his skin and the feel of her soft, rounded body against him and he wanted to drown himself in her body. There was no going back now.

Diana was finally beginning to gather the strength to resist where this was going. It was so hard to push away the man she'd wanted close for most of her life but she knew she had to do it. She couldn't believe, after all she'd been through, after all the serious thinking she'd done on the subject and all the serious preparations she'd made to resist her feelings toward him, here she was, lost in his kiss and loving it. How could this be?

Maybe her response to the temptation that was Cam was so strong because it had been so long since a man had held her and kissed her…but no, it wasn't a man's touch she craved. It was Cam's touch. Only Cam.

She finally mustered the force to pull away from him, leaning back, still in his arms.

"Oh, Cam," she said in despair, her gaze taking in his beautiful face and loving it.

"Hush," he whispered, leaning forward to drop a kiss on her neck. "Unless you want Janey bursting in here to demand an explanation."

She sighed, shaking her head. "Admit it. This isn't working."

He kissed her collarbone. "What isn't working?"

Reaching up, she pushed hard to make him release her. "Our plan to stay away from each other."

He looked amused. "Hey, don't try to pin that plan on me. I never liked it much anyway."

Her sigh was a heartfelt sign of regret. "I thought once I told you face-to-face…"

"That didn't work, did it? Want to try something else?"

"What?"

"This." He leaned closer again and began to nibble on her ear.

She pushed him away. "No! Cam, we have to try harder."

"Hold on." He shook his head, looking down at her in disbelief. "Di, you need to decide what you really want. You order me out of your life, then show up in my bedroom. Either you've developed a split personality, or you're conflicted in some way."

"I was just delivering flowers," she said plaintively, knowing it wasn't going to fly as a serious defense.

"Ah, the old delivering flowers ploy."

"Cam, I didn't mean to start anything like this."

"Didn't you?"

"I thought you were gone."

"You were wrong."

"Obviously." She managed to get a little more space between them, her gaze lingering on his wide shoulders and the beautiful planes of his naked chest. Just looking at him made her stomach do a flip and made her knees begin to tremble. She had to get away from him quickly or she was going to be lost. She closed her eyes and pressed her lips together, then opened them again with more determination. "Now how am I going to get out of here without running into your sister?"

"I heard her go back downstairs a minute ago. You should be in the clear."

She stared at him. She hadn't heard anyone go by again. She'd been deep into kissing him, too deep to be able to process anything else. But he hadn't been, had he? That was something to keep in mind.

Turning away from him, she gathered her supplies,

her hands shaking and fingers trembling, and headed for the door. He pulled it open for her and smiled.

"Give me a minute and I'll get dressed and…"

"No." She shook her head. "I'm going, Cam. This doesn't change anything."

His eyes darkened. "The hell it doesn't," he muttered.

She shook her head again, looking out into the hall to make sure it was clear. "Goodbye," she said. Avoiding his gaze, she hurried away.

She made a quick trip through the first floor rooms, giving her arrangements a last-minute check, then turned to leave and almost ran into Janey.

"Hello." Cam's sister was dressed in a black leotard with a bright pink sweatshirt worn over it. Her hair was up in foil, being colorized. Diana quickly made the assessment that the voice she'd heard in the hallway was her hairdresser. She knew the woman came to the house on a weekly basis.

"I saw your car," Janey said. "I was wondering where you were."

"I was putting flowers in a number of rooms," Diana said, trying hard to sound innocent and casual. "And I'm running late."

Janey's green eyes flickered. "Well, how's that baby coming?" she asked.

Something in her tone put Diana on alert. "Just fine, thank you," she said, looking at Janey hard before starting for the kitchen.

To her surprise, Janey stepped forward and blocked the doorway, looking at her speculatively. "You know, there are people who have practically come out and asked me if Cam is the father."

Diana's heart lurched but she stood her ground. "How interesting. Too bad you don't know the answer, isn't it?" She felt a twinge of regret. Why didn't she just tell the woman Cam wasn't the father and put the question to bed? But hadn't Cam already tried to do that? Janey wouldn't believe her no matter what she said.

"Mother is still planning her parties," Janey said coolly, her eyes flashing. "You do understand what these parties are about, don't you?"

"I think I have a vague idea."

Janey nodded. "We need Cam to marry a rich girl. That's pretty much our only hope of getting out of our current financial difficulties."

Diana held her anger in check, but it wasn't easy. "Good luck to you," she said, and stepped forward in a way that signaled she wanted to go through the doorway.

Janey didn't move out of the way, but her eyes narrowed. "So tell me, how does that fit in with your plans, exactly?"

She glanced down at Diana's rounded belly, making it very clear what she was talking about. She was worried that Diana was going to try to snag Cam for herself. Diana's anger was truly simmering now. How dare she! Well, she could just go on wondering. No matter what she was told, she wasn't going to believe it.

"I don't have any plans, Janey," she said, meeting the other woman's gaze with her own clear vision.

Janey arched an eyebrow. "Don't you?"

"No." She arched an eyebrow in return. "In fact, the parties are going to have to go on without me. I'm going out of town for a while. So you're going to have to find someone else to try to bully." With one firm hand, she gently pushed a surprised Janey out of the doorway and made it past her. "So long."

She walked quickly through the kitchen and out to her car, swearing softly to herself as she went. That woman!

It wasn't until she was in the driver's seat and starting the engine that she remembered what she'd said to her and she half laughed.

So she was going out of town. Funny, she hadn't realized she had a trip in her future until she'd told Janey. But now that it was out in the open, she was glad she'd thought of it. It was probably her only hope to stay away from Cam. And with a little distance and a bit of perspective, she might even think of a way to fall out of love with him.

CHAPTER SIX

DIANA was back in town.

She'd been gone a little over a week. She'd left her occasional assistant, Penny, in charge of supplying arrangements to her weekly clients, and she'd spent a few days in San Francisco with her old roommates.

She'd made a run up to Sacramento as well, hoping to catch her cousin, Ben, but he was gone on business, so she missed him. They had since connected by phone and he was coming to Gold Dust today so they could meet. He had some things to show her.

She was very curious as to what he was up to. Having her uncle leave them a piece of property together was interesting but she wasn't sure if that wasn't going to be more trouble than it was worth. Hopefully Ben would clear some of this up when he arrived.

They were meeting at Dorry's Café on Main and she was on her way there now. She lucked into a good parking place in front of the library under a big old magnolia tree. It was a short walk to the café, but she needed the exercise.

She had a lot of things on her mind, but mostly, she was thinking about Cam. Had absence made the heart grow fonder? Not really. She couldn't get much fonder. But there definitely had been no "out of sight, out of mind" involved, either. Thinking about Cam sometimes seemed to be her main state of being. She was getting better and better at it. And it had to stop.

But there was something else on her mind as well—or should she say someone else? She could feel Mia move, just a flutter, like a butterfly caught in a magic net, but that tiny bit of movement made all the difference. Mia was real to her now like she hadn't been before. Mia was her baby, her child, the center of her future and that meant that Mia was all the world to her.

She was definitely showing, and proud of it. But that made for a different atmosphere as she walked down the streets of the little Sierra town she'd lived in all her life and interacted with the people. Strangely she felt almost as though someone had painted a big red A on her chest when she wasn't paying attention. Suddenly everyone was noticing that she was carrying a child, and most of the looks she was getting were not sympathetic.

Still, what she saw wasn't really old-fashioned small town disapproval. What she had to face every day was even more annoying—blatant curiosity. Everyone wanted to know who the father was. They all knew very well that she hadn't dated anyone for over a year. She had taken a few trips to San Francisco, but other than that, she was busy working with her flowers and hanging out at her lake, with nary a male in sight.

Of course, things were different now. Cam was back.

And it seemed Janey wasn't the only one with suspicions. It was amazing how many ways people could contort a simple conversation into hinting around at the question—*was the baby Cam's?*

Everyone knew that Cam had been her champion once upon a time. Now she was pregnant—and he was back. Was there a connection? It was difficult to find a way to come right out and tell them there was nothing to the rumors when they never actually put the darn thing into words she could refute. They just said something here and left a little hint there and gave her looks that spoke volumes.

She was working on a way to deal with the problem without getting too rude, but as time passed and more and more people got bolder and bolder with their probing, she was beginning to think rude might be the only way to go.

But she smiled and nodded to passersby as she made her way to Dorry's. Maybe this was just the price you had to pay for living in a small town. And bottom line— she loved it here.

Cam saw her going into Dorry's and he stopped on the street to have a two-minute argument with himself. He knew she didn't want to see him or talk to him, but the fact was, he wanted very much to see her and they had plenty of things to discuss. She'd been gone for a week and he'd missed her. That morning in his bedroom had proven one thing—she wanted him. The fact that he wanted her was a given. But no matter how she protested, she'd let the cat out of the bag, so to speak. Left to its own devices, her body would take him in a New York minute. It was just her heart and mind he had to convince.

Just thinking about that morning made him throb and he knew it was going to be very hard to stay away from her. He wanted to talk to her. Hell, he wanted to be with her. Should he leave her alone, give her a few more days of peace? Or should he get on with this?

They were friends, first and foremost. He valued her like he had valued few others in his life. And from the moment he'd seen her the other night, a new element had been added. Of course she knew that. He hadn't been very subtle about it. She attracted him in every way possible.

But he wasn't a nut case. He knew she was out of bounds right now and he respected her need to stay away from him most of the time. He didn't agree with it and he didn't like it, but he had every intention of keeping his distance—for the moment. Until he convinced her it was pointless.

But did running into her here in town count? Not at all, he decided at last. After all, this was casual and public and totally nonthreatening. So he might as well go on in and say hello.

Great. That was settled. He strode confidently toward the café and went in, waving to plump, friendly Dorry with her head of gray curls and nodding to Jim, the tall, skinny mechanic who had worked on fixing his car and was now up to his elbows in a big, juicy cheeseburger. But all the time, he was searching for a familiar looking blonde.

And there she was.

"Hey, good-lookin'," he said, sliding into the booth across from her and smiling.

She looked up and winced. It was like looking into the sun. The light from the big bay window shone all around him, giving him a halo effect. That, along with his dazzling smile, sent her reeling for a split second or two. He was too gorgeous to be real. Maybe she'd just invented him in her head.

Everything about him looked smooth and clean, from the tanned skin showed off by his open shirt, to his beautiful, long-fingered hands. For a moment, she thought she'd lost the ability to breathe. Whenever she saw him unprepared, he made her react this way. No other man had ever affected her like this. Why oh why? It just wasn't fair.

"Go away," she said hopefully, but there was no strength of will behind her words.

"No," he said calmly. "You've admitted that we are friends. Old friends. Dear friends. And friends get together now and then and shoot the breeze. That's what we're doing here."

She raised her gaze to the ceiling and said plaintively, "It would be better if you would go away."

"We're adults, Di," he said pleasantly as he reached across and took a bread stick from the basket the waitress had put on the table. "We can sit in a café and talk."

She looked worried. "Can we?"

He grinned and waved the bread stick at her. "You bet."

Diana shivered and shook her head, trying to ground

herself and get back to reality. "Some other time, maybe," she said, and as she said it she seemed to pick up confidence. "I don't have time today. I'm meeting someone."

"Oh?" He tensed and his sense of humor seemed to evaporate without a trace. Suddenly he was very guarded.

"You'll have to leave before he gets here."

So the person she was waiting for was male, was he? Cam stared across the table at her. She looked nervous. Her usual calm was not evident and her hands were fluttering as they pushed her hair back behind her ear, then reached for her glass of water, then dropped back into her lap. Was he making her nervous? Or was it the pending arrival of her visitor?

He went very still and stared at the wall. His first guess was that this was the father of her baby whom she was meeting in this public place. Had to be. In which case he wasn't leaving until he got a good look at him.

He turned his gaze back and met hers squarely. "Diana, I'm going to be up-front about this. My instincts are to throw you over my shoulder and run off to a cave for the duration."

Diana had unfortunately just taken a drink of water and she nearly spewed it across the room. "What are you talking about?" she sputtered hoarsely, still choking on the water as she leaned across the table in hopes no one else would hear this.

"I'm serious." He leaned forward, too, speaking as softly as he could, but with definite emphasis, and gazing at her intently. "I want to take care of you. I want to protect you. I want to make sure you and your baby are okay." He grabbed her hand and held it. "Everything in me is aching to do that. And I have to know." He grimaced. "Are you going to marry this guy?"

She blinked at him. "What guy?" she asked in bewilderment.

"The father of your baby. Mia's father."

"Mia's… Oh, Cam." She almost laughed, but not quite, and her fingers curled around his and then her eyes were suddenly shimmering with unshed tears. "You're crazy."

His hand tightened on hers. "That doesn't answer my question."

"Who says I have to give you an answer?" She smiled through her tears. "But I will. No, I'm not going to marry anyone. I'm like you. No wedding in my future."

He set his jaw with resolution and looked deep into her eyes. "Okay," he said. "Then I'm warning you, I'm going to do what I have to do."

"As long as you leave me with my feet on the ground," she teased him. "And no caves, okay?"

He shrugged. "Like I said, I'll do what I have to."

The waitress arriving with the salad she'd ordered saved Diana from having to respond to that. She drew back and sat up straight and looked across the table at Cam. She couldn't help but love him for his concern for her and her baby. Still, that didn't change anything.

But this was no place to have that argument. As soon as the waitress was gone again, she picked up a fork and began to pick at her food, and meanwhile, she changed the subject.

"Your mother was on my answering machine twice in the last few days. I'm going to have to call her back eventually. What am I going to say to her?"

His wide mouth twisted. "A warm hello would be nice, I suppose."

She studied his face. "Have you told her yet? Does she understand that you aren't going to be doing the parties?"

Leaning back, he sighed and looked troubled. "I have told her as firmly as I can muster. What she understands and doesn't understand is another matter."

"Meaning?"

"Meaning she is so deep in denial…" He straightened and rubbed his neck. "Well, I did try to have it out with her yesterday. I'm afraid there was a little yelling."

She put down her fork and stared at him. "You didn't yell at your mother!"

He grimaced. "Just a little bit." He definitely looked sheepish. "She drives me crazy. She just won't face reality."

"Didn't you show her some documentation? Facts and figures? Spreadsheets and accounting forms?"

He nodded. "Even an eviction notice."

"What?"

"For one of our warehouses in Sacramento."

"Oh." She sagged with relief. The picture of Mrs. Van Kirk being carted out of her home by the sheriff with an eviction notice was a nightmare scenario she didn't want to see played out in the flesh.

"But I showed it to her to try to convince her of how serious this is. Well, she got a little hysterical and ran out to go to her precious rose garden and fell right down the garden steps."

Diana's hands went to her face in horror. "No! How is she?"

Cam was looking so guilty, she couldn't help but feel sorry for him, even though she knew his mother probably deserved the pity more.

"She was pretty shaken up." He sighed with regret. "And she broke her ankle."

"What?"

He shook his head, his eyes filled with tragedy. "All my fault, of course."

"Oh, poor thing."

He gave her a halfhearted smile. "I knew you would understand."

"Not you! Your mother." But she knew he was only trying to lighten the mood with a joke, and his quick grin confirmed that.

"Don't worry. It's a hairline fracture sort of thing. The orthopedist said she'll be better in about a month and good as new by Christmas."

Diana groaned. "She's got a hard row to hoe," she said. "It's hard sitting still when you're used to being busy all the time."

"True." He looked at her speculatively. "So now we're reversing a lot of plans," he went on more seriously. "We're firing a lot of the workmen she hired and we're letting the caterer from San Francisco go. And the rose expert. And the barbecue center will have to wait for flusher times."

Diana sighed, shaking her head. "I suppose you'll be laying off the floral stylist as well, won't you?"

"Is that what you call yourself?"

She nodded.

He grinned without much humor. "Yup, she's a goner."

Diana sighed again. "Your mother's been my best account."

He gave her his finest cynical sneer. "Such are the ripples in a stagnating pond."

She laughed. "Now that's just downright silly," she told him. "The Van Kirks are not stagnating. I thought you were going to see to that."

He nodded, his eyes brimming with laughter. That was one thing he loved about her, she seemed to get his silly jokes and actually to enjoy them. Not many people could say that.

"I'm doing what I can. I still can't say we've saved the house. But I'm working at it."

"I'm sure you are." She gave him a quelling look. "Now if you would just buckle down and marry some rich gal, all would be forgiven."

"Right."

"But if you're not going to have the parties…"

He frowned uncomfortably. "Well, about the parties…"

"Yes?" she said, one eyebrow arched in surprise.

He made a face. "We're sort of compromising."

"What does that mean?"

"She was so devastated, I had to give her something. So there will just be one party. A simple party. No fancy chefs, no rose experts."

"I see."

"Mother, Janey and Rosa are going to have to do most of the work themselves." He hesitated, narrowed his eyes and gazed at her as though evaluating her mood. "But since she's flat on her back right now, we need a coordinator to take charge."

Diana's head rose. Why hadn't she seen this coming from farther away? She knew she was staring at him like a deer in the headlights. She was thinking as fast as she could to find excuses for saying no to him. She had to say no. A yes would be emotional suicide.

She could just imagine what it would be like, watching beautiful young, rich ladies from the foremost families in the foothills, dressed in skimpy summer frocks, vying for Cam's attention while she was dressed like a French maid, passing the crudités. No, thank you!

"Janey could do it," she suggested quickly.

"Sure she could," he said out of the corner of his mouth. "If we want a disaster to rival the Titanic. She'll undermine it all she can." He gave her a significant look. "There's only one person Mother would trust to handle this."

She stared back at him. "You can't be thinking what I'm thinking you're thinking."

He shrugged and looked hopeful. "Why not?"

Slowly she began to shake her head. "You couldn't pay me enough. And anyway, didn't you say you were broke?"

He nodded. "That's why I'm hoping you'll do it for free."

She laughed aloud at his raw audacity. "There is no

way I'm going to do this at all. Save your breath, Mr. Van Kirk. I refuse to have anything to do with the whole thing."

This could have gone on and on if it hadn't been for the arrival of Diana's visitor. He stopped by their booth, a tall man, handsome in a gaunt way, just starting to gray at the temples, and dressed in an expensive suit. Cam hated him on sight.

"Hello, Diana," he said, smiling coolly.

"Oh." Diana had to readjust quickly. "Hi, Ben. Uh, this is my friend Cam." She threw out a pointed glance. "He was just leaving."

Cam didn't budge. He made a show of looking at his watch. "Actually I think I've got a little more time."

"Cam!"

"And I've got a sudden yen for a piece of Dorry's apple pie. It's been ten years, but I can still remember that delicate crust she used to make."

She glared at him, and so did Ben, but Cam smiled sunnily and went on as though he hadn't noticed the bad vibes, chattering about pie and apples and good old home cookin'.

"Cam," Diana said firmly at last. "Ben and I have something personal to discuss. You've got to go."

He gazed at her intently. "Are you sure?" he said softly, searching her eyes. He wanted to make certain she really meant it, that she didn't want him to stay and act as a buffer for her.

She gave him a look that should have warned him that she was losing patience. "I'm sure. Please go."

He rose reluctantly and flashed her friend a sharp

look, just to let him know he was going to be keeping an eye on him.

"Okay," he said. "I'll be over there in the corner, eating apple pie. In case you need me."

She closed her eyes and waited for him to go. Ben looked bored. Cam went.

But he didn't go far and he kept up his survey of what was going on from a pretty good vantagepoint. They were talking earnestly, leaning so that their heads were close together over the table. It tore him up to watch them. If this was really the guy…

Their meeting didn't last very long. Ben pulled out a portfolio of papers that he showed her, but he packed most of them away again and was obviously preparing to leave. Cam felt a sense of relief. There had been nothing warm between them, none of the sort of gestures people who had an emotional bond might display. If there had ever been anything between them, he would say it was pretty much dead now. In fact, Diana looked almost hostile as Ben rose to leave. And as soon as he was out of sight, she looked up and nodded to Cam, as though to beckon to him. He was already up and moving and he went to her immediately, sliding in where the other man had been sitting.

"I need your help," she said without preamble. She had one piece of paper that he'd left behind sitting on the table in front of her. "Because I don't know how to do this."

"Do what?" he asked. "Sue the guy? Charge him with abandonment? Get some money out of him for child care?"

She was shaking her head, wearing a puzzled frown. "What are you talking about?"

He blinked. "That wasn't the father of your baby?"

She threw her head back. "Oh, Cam, for heaven's sake! Ben is my cousin. I told you about him."

"You did?" Her cousin. It figured. The body language had been all wrong for lovers, or even current enemies who were past lovers. He should have known. Feeling a little foolish, but even more relieved, he took a deep breath and calmed down. "Oh. Maybe you did."

"Never mind that," she said, staring down at the paper. "Here's the deal. Ben's a lawyer. He always seems to be looking for a weak spot to exploit." She looked up, wrinkling her nose. "You know what I mean? Our uncle Luke, my father's older brother, died last week. I met him a few times years ago and he came to my father's funeral. But to my shock, he had a little piece of land in the mountains and he left it to Ben and me."

"The two of you together?" That could be a seemingly lucky break but with a sword of Damocles hanging over it.

"Yes. I assume he thought we would sell it and share the revenue or one would buy the other out. Whatever."

"Okay. What's the problem?"

She frowned, chewing her lip. "Ben wants to buy me out. But…" She made a face, thought for a moment, then leaned closer, speaking softly. "I know this is going to sound really horrible, but I don't trust him. Everything he says seems logical enough and it sounds good and all. But, well, he tried to find a way to get a piece of my lake property when my dad died. He wasn't all that open about it, but I could tell he was snooping around here for a purpose. And now I just can't help but wonder…"

"Better safe than sorry," he agreed. "Where's the land?"

"That's just it. He seems a little vague about that. He does say it's out in the sticks, far from any amenities and there seem to be some encumbrances on it that are going to make things difficult. I did get something in the mail myself, something from my uncle's lawyer, but I couldn't make heads nor tails of it and when I tried to call him, the number didn't seem to work. Ben gave me this paper with the parcel number and coordinates, but as far as a map on how to get there, he was very unhelpful."

"Has he been out to take a look at it?"

"He says he has. He says it's pretty barren. Flatland with not even a lot of vegetation. No views. Nothing."

Cam nodded, thinking that over. "So you're a bit skeptical."

She made a face. "I hate to say it, but yes. Color me skeptical."

"And you would like to go take a look for yourself." He nodded again, assessing things. "I think that's good. You need to know a little more about where it is and what condition it's in before you make any drastic moves."

"I think so," she said. "For all I know, it's a garden paradise or a great site to build a house on." She squinted at him hopefully. "I just thought you might know what state or county agencies to go to and things like that. Or maybe you have connections in the Forest Service?"

"I know some people who might be able to help." He

looked over the paper for another moment. "Can I take this with me?"

"Of course."

"Good." He folded it and put it in his pocket, then gave her a sardonic look. "I'm going to have to pull some strings, you know. I might have to call in some favors. Use my family's influence." His smile was suddenly wicked. "And after I've done all that, going out of my way, putting my reputation on the line, going all out to do something for you…" His shrug was teasingly significant. "Well, I'm sure you're going to be more open to doing a favor for me in return."

It was obvious he was still trying to get her to manage the party for his mother—the last thing on earth she wanted to do.

"Cam!"

His wide mouth turned down at the corners for just a moment. "Just think about it. That's all I ask." He patted the paper in his pocket. "I'll get back to you on this." His smile returned to being warm and natural. "You'll trust me?"

"Of course I'll trust you." She smiled back at him. It just wasn't possible not to. "Now go away," she said.

Actually he was late for a meeting at the mayor's office, so for once he obeyed her. But first, he leaned forward, caught her hand in his and brought it to his lips, kissing her palm.

"See you later," he promised, giving her a melting look.

She shook her head, half-laughing at him as he slid out and left the café. But as she looked around the room at the glances she was getting, her face got very hot. It was obvious a lot of people had witnessed that hand kissing thing and could hardly wait to get on their cell phones to tell their friends what they'd seen.

Small towns!

CHAPTER SEVEN

IT ONLY took Cam two days to get all the information Diana needed to make a trek up to see the land. She was thrilled when he called her with the news. So now she'd fed the kitten and watered her flower garden and dressed herself in hiking clothes and was ready to go. This was totally an adventure and she was looking forward to it. She just had to wait for Cam to show up with the map of the location of where she was going.

She knew she was not acting according to plan. She'd sworn she was going to stay away from Cam—far, far away. She wasn't going to risk falling back into the patterns that had ruled her life for so long. She was a grown woman with a child on the way and she couldn't afford to act like a lovesick teenager.

She knew asking for his help put her in a weaker position in refusing to help his mother, and yet, she'd done it anyway. Somehow Cam kept weaving his way through the threads of her days, finding a reason here, an excuse there, and before she knew it, she was almost back in the fold, tangled in his life, loving him again, unable to imagine a future without him.

It had to stop. Right after he gave her the map. She had the grace to laugh out loud as she had that thought. What a ridiculous fool she was!

She heard his car and hurried out to meet him, hoping to get the map and send him on his way. He got out of the car and leaned against it, watching her come toward him with a look of pleasure on his face. She couldn't help but smile.

"Oh, Cam, don't do that."

"Don't do what? Enjoy you?"

She gave him a look. "Do you have the map?"

"Yes, I do."

She looked at him. Both hands were empty.

"Where is it?"

"In the car."

"Oh." She tried to look around him. "May I have it?"

"No."

She stared at him. "What do you mean?"

His eyes sparkled in the sun. "I'm the keeper of the map. I'll handle all navigational duties."

She put her hands on her hips and gave him a mock glare. "That'll be a little hard to do, since you'll be here and I'll be the one approaching the site," she said crisply.

"Au contraire," he countered smugly. "Since we're going in my car…"

"No way!"

"And I have the picnic prepared by Rosa this very

morning and packed away in an awesome picnic basket, with accoutrements for two."

She drew in a quick breath. "I never said you could come with me."

He gave her the patented lopsided grin that so often had young ladies swooning in the aisles. "That's right, you never did. But I'm coming anyway."

Fighting this was probably a losing battle and not worth the effort as it stood, but still, she frowned, trying to think of a way out. "Can I just see the map?"

"Sure. But I'll hold it."

She groaned at his lack of trust, but that was forgotten as he spread out the map and showed her where her property lay.

"Ohmigosh, that's really far from any main roads. I thought it would be closer to Lake Tahoe."

"It's uncharted territory. Just be glad it's not winter. Think about the Donner party."

She shuddered. "No, thanks." She frowned at him, trying to be fierce. "Now if you'll just give me the map."

He smiled and dropped a sudden, unexpected kiss on her forehead. "I go with the map. Take it or leave it."

She shook her head, but a slight smile was teasing her lips and her heart was beating just a little faster. "What a bully you are."

"Guilty as charged. Let's go."

They went.

It was a lovely drive through the foothills and then into the taller mountains. They passed through small idyllic towns on the way, and little enclaves of farm or ranch houses. Cows, horses and alpacas seemed to be grazing everywhere on the still-green grasses. They talked and laughed and pointed out the sights, and all in all, had a very good time. The final segment was a fifteen-mile ride on a dirt road and that was another story. For almost half an hour, they were bouncing so hard, conversation was impossible.

And then they arrived. Cam brought the car to a stop in a cloud of dust and they both sat there, staring out at the open area. For a moment or two, neither said a word.

Finally Diana asked pitifully, "Are you sure this is it?"

"Afraid so," he said.

She turned to gaze at him, a look of irony in her eyes. "I don't think there could be an uglier patch of land in all the Sierras, do you?"

"It's definitely an ugly little spud," he said out of the side of his mouth, shaking his head. "I don't think anyone is going to want to build here. There are no trees, no view, no nothing."

"No paved road," she pointed out, wincing as she looked back at all the rocks and gullies they were going to have to go back through. "Looks like the best thing to do would be to take Ben up on his offer and let him buy me out."

"Maybe." Cam frowned, leaning forward on the steering wheel. "Though I can't help wondering why he wants it—or whom he's going to sell it to. I can't see one redeeming element here."

She let out a sigh. "Darn. I was hoping for a bit of good luck for a change."

"Ya gotta make your own luck, sweetheart," Cam said in his best Sam Spade imitation. "That's the way the game is played."

She made a face at him and admitted, "I don't even see a place to have a picnic here. And we passed a nice park about thirty minutes ago. Shall we go back?"

The ride back wasn't any better than the ride out had been, but they found their way to the nice park and sighed with relief when they got there. The park had tables with built-in benches and they set up their feast on a nice one under an oak, in full view of the small river that ran through the area. Rosa's lunch was delicious. They ate and talked softly in the noon day sunshine. A group of children played tag a short distance away. Mothers with strollers passed, cooing to their babies.

Diana took a bite of her chicken salad sandwich as she watched the passing parade. "Funny how, once you're pregnant, you suddenly notice all the babies that pop up everywhere."

He gave her a covert look. She'd brought up her pregnancy on her own. Did this mean that the moratorium on mentioning it was lifted? Just in case, he made sure to tread softly.

"You're going to make a great mom," he noted.

She flashed him a look and for a moment, he thought he was going to get his head handed to him. But then her face softened and she almost smiled.

"What makes you say that?" she asked.

"I get a clear vibe from you that seems encouraging,"

he said. "You seem to be settling into this new role you're about to play in the world."

Now a smile was definitely tugging at the corners of her mouth. "It's funny, but it has taken me a while to fully realize what I've done, what I'm about to do. Mia seems very real to me now. I can hardly wait to hold her in my arms. I only hope I'll be a good mother to her."

"I have no doubts. I remember how you took care of your father."

"Do you?" She looked at him in surprise, then with growing appreciation. "I don't think most people remember that, or even noticed at the time." She shook her head. She'd spent too much of her young life taking care of him and getting little thanks for it. But she'd done it out of duty and a feeling of compassion for the man. And though she'd gone off to the big city as soon as she could, to leave all that behind her, she'd come back when her father needed her and no one else would have taken care of him as he lay dying. So she did it.

Funny. She'd left Gold Dust because of her father and then she'd returned for the same reason.

"He needed someone to take care of him. It was a cinch he couldn't take care of himself."

He waved a carrot stick at her. "You were taking care of him when you were too young to be taking care of anything more than whether your socks matched."

She smiled. Trust Cam to have paid attention and to have realized how difficult it was for her when she was young. How could you not fall for a guy like that?

She was quiet for a moment, then said softly, "I loved him, you know."

He looked at her and saw the clouds in her eyes. He wanted to take her in his arms, but he held off, knowing how she felt about the situation.

"Of course you did. He was your father." He shifted in his seat. "Did you ever know your mother at all?"

"Not much." She shook her head. "She took off before I was six years old and never looked back."

"That's a shame."

She tilted her head back and smoothed her hair off her face. "I'm not so sure. If she was worth knowing, she'd have made a point of letting me know her." Her laugh was short and spiked with irony. "At least my father stuck around."

They packed away the remnants of their lunch, put things into the car, and walked down to watch the river roll by. There were just enough boulders and flat rocks in the river's path to make for a pretty spectacular water show. They followed the river for a bit, then sat on a large rock and listened to the rushing sound.

"You need something like this at your place," he told her. "Your lake could use some shaking up."

"I've got a nice stream," she protested. "That's more my sort of excitement. Something manageable and contained."

He laughed, leaning back beside her and tossing a flat pebble into the river. "That's all you want out of life, is it? Something manageable?"

"What's wrong with that?"

"Not a thing." He tossed another pebble. "But back about the time I left, I thought you had plans to go to the city and become a model." He shifted so that she could lean back against his shoulder instead of the hard rock. "What happened to that?"

She hesitated, then gave in to temptation and let her body snuggle in against his. "Kid dreams," she said airily.

He turned his head, savoring the feel of her against him. A sudden breeze tossed her hair against his face and he breathed in her spicy scent. "You would've been good," he said, closing his eyes as he took in the sense of her.

"No."

"Why not?" Opening his eyes again, he was almost indignant. "You've got the bones for it. You could be a model." Reaching out, he touched her hair, then turned his hand, gathering up the strands like reins on a wonderful pony. "You…Diana, you're beautiful."

He said it as though it were the revelation of the ages. She smiled wryly, appreciating his passion but knowing it was just a bit biased.

"I'm not cut out for that sort of life," she said simply.

"Chicken."

She shook her head. "No. It's not that."

He went very still for a moment, thinking over her situation. "Maybe you should have gone for it anyway," he said softly.

She moved impatiently, turning to look at him. "You don't understand. I know more about it than you think I do. I lived in San Francisco for a couple of years after college. I did all those things you do when you live in

San Francisco. I went to parties in bay-view penthouses, danced in sleazy discos, dated young account executives and overworked law students. Climbed halfway to the stars in little cable cars. Lived on a houseboat in Sausalito for a few months. Worked at a boring job. Had my car broken into. Had my apartment robbed. Had a lot of fun but finally I'd had enough and I wanted to come home. To me cities are kind of those 'great to visit but don't make me live there' sorts of places."

He smiled, enjoying how caught up in her subject she'd become. Reaching up, he touched her cheek. "You're just a small town girl at heart."

"I guess so. I love it in Gold Dust." She threw her head back, thinking of it. "I love to wake up in the morning and see the breeze ruffling the surface of the lake. I love the wind high up in the pines and the fresh smell after a rainstorm. I love that feeling of calm as the sun sinks behind the mountaintops and changes the atmosphere into a magic twilight."

"I understand," he said. "That's part of what pulled at me to come back." He hesitated only a few beats. "That…and you."

The moment he said it, he knew it was true. Through all the turmoil, all the hell he'd gone through with Gina, Diana had always been in the back of his mind, a calm, rational presence, an angel of mercy whose care could heal his soul. He'd always pushed the memories away, thinking they were a crutch he'd held on to in order to comfort himself, like a favorite fantasy. But now he knew it was much more. What he felt for Diana might be fairly hopeless, but it was real and true and strong inside him. It was more real than any other part of his life had ever been. His gaze slid over her, searching the shadowed areas along her neckline, her collarbone, the upper swell of her breasts.

She turned toward him slowly, as though in a dream. She knew he was going to kiss her. She heard it in his voice. Her heart was thumping so loud, she wasn't sure if she could breathe. He was going to kiss her and once again, just for this moment, she was going to kiss him back.

She didn't wait, but leaned toward him, her lips already parted, and his arms came around her and she clung to him, moving in a cloud of sensual happiness. Was this real? Was that really Cam's body that felt so warm and wonderful against hers?

It was over too soon. She sighed as he pulled back, then smiled up at him.

"How can I miss you if you won't go away?" she murmured, half-laughing.

"What is that supposed to mean?" he asked, touching her cheek with his forefinger.

"It means you're always there," she said, straightening and moving away from him. "You're either in my life or in my dreams. I can't get rid of you." She said it lightly, as though teasing, but she meant every word.

He watched her through narrowed eyes, wondering why she appealed to him more than any other woman he'd ever known. Holding her felt natural, kissing her had been magic. He wanted her in his bed, in his life. But what did that signify? Right now, it was just confusing.

It was later, as they winged their way home, that he brought up the topic she'd been dreading all along.

"You haven't been over to the house for a while."

"No. I was gone and then…" She let her voice taper off because she knew there was no good excuse for her sending Penny to take care of the arrangements at the Van Kirk mansion one more time, even though she herself was back in town.

"My mother is asking that you come see her," he said, glancing at her sideways.

"Oh, no," Diana said, her eyes full of dread. "She's going to beg me to take over the party plans, isn't she?"

He nodded. "Yes."

She wrinkled her nose. "Tell her I've got the flu."

This time his look was on the scathing side. "I make it a practice never to lie to women," he said, and she wasn't sure if he was joking or not.

She smiled sadly just the same. "Only to men, huh?"

He suppressed a quick grin. "Of course. A man can handle a lie. Likely as not, he'll appreciate a well-told one. Might even appropriate it for his own use in the future, and thank you for it, besides."

"Unlike a woman," she countered teasingly.

"Women only appreciate lies about themselves, and then only if they're complimentary."

She stared at him, struck by how serious he sounded all of a sudden. "What made you so cynical about the human race?" she asked him.

For just a moment he was tempted to tell her about Gina, the only other woman he'd been close to loving over the last ten years, about how she'd nearly pulled him into an ugly trap, teaching him a lesson about feminine lying he would never forget. But at the last moment, he decided it was a story best kept to himself and he passed over it. It was all very well to use episodes from the past as lessons in guarding one's trust like a stingy uncle, but to inflict those stories on others was probably too much.

"Life does take its toll," he said lightly instead.

"Are you done?" she asked.

He glanced at her in surprise. "Done doing what?"

"Done running around the world looking for affirmation."

He gave a cough of laughter. "Is that what I've been doing? And here I thought I was looking for adventure all this time."

She shrugged, loving the way his hair curled around his ear, loving the line of his profile, loving him in every way she possibly could. She'd missed him so. She would miss him again when he left. And she was sure his leaving was inevitable. She didn't know when, but she knew he would go. And this time, she refused to let her heart break over it.

"Tell me why you went in the first place? The real reason."

"You mean, beyond the fight with my grandfather? It's pretty simple. The age-old story." He maneuvered through a traffic circle in the little city they were passing through. "I had to go to see if I could make it on my own without the Van Kirk name boosting me along. I didn't

want to end up like my father. And I didn't much want
to end up like my grandfather, either. I wanted to be me."

She nodded. That was pretty much what she'd
expected. "And now?"

He grinned. "Now I'm thinking my grandfather isn't
such a bad model after all."

"Interesting." She thought about that for a moment,
then went on. "Has anyone ever told you that a lot of
people thought you left because of Lulu?" she informed
him, watching for his reaction.

He looked blank. "Lulu?"

"Lulu. Lulu Borden. You remember her." She hid her
smile.

"Oh, sure. Tall, curvy girl. Lots of red hair. Nice
smile. Kind of flirty."

"That's Lulu."

He shrugged. "What does Lulu have to do with me?"

"Well…" She gave him an arch look. "She started
showing right about the time you disappeared. A lot of
people figured you were the one who got her that way.
And that was why you took off."

"What?" He gaped at her in horror until she reminded
him to keep his eyes on the road. "If a lot of people
thought that a lot of people were wrong."

She nodded happily. "I was pretty sure of that, but
it's good to hear you confirm it."

He frowned, still bothered by the charge against him.
"What did Lulu have to say about it?"

"She married Tommy Hunsucker, so she's not
sayin' much."

"Geesh." He shook his head with a look of infinite sadness. "Maligned in my own hometown."

"Sure," she said cheerfully. "Where better to have your reputation besmirched?"

"And now they think I'm a daddy again, don't they?" he said cynically, looking at her growing tummy. "At least the town has a lot of faith in my potency."

She grinned. "Legends speak louder than facts sometimes," she admitted.

"Speaking of legends…" He hesitated, then went on bravely. "Tell me why you aren't going to marry the father of your baby."

All the humor drained from her face and she seemed to freeze. "That is not up for discussion."

He turned to look at her. "Di…"

"No. I'm not going to tell you anything." She shook her head emphatically and her tone was more than firm. "This is my baby. The father has nothing to do with it."

He winced. "That's not true."

"It is true," she insisted fiercely. "That's it." She held her hand up. "End of discussion."

He didn't press it any further, but he thought about it all the rest of the way home.

It was late afternoon before they turned onto the Gold Dust Road and came in sight of her little house by the lake.

"Getting back to the point," he said as he pulled up before her gate. "Will you go to see my mother?"

"Wow, that was a subject I thought we'd left in the dust way back there somewhere. Or at least we should have."

She thought for a moment before answering. She

wanted to give him the benefit of the doubt, an even chance, a fair hearing, and all those other tired clichés that meant he probably had a point to make and she ought to let him make it.

He moved impatiently. He obviously thought she'd taken enough time to come up with a fair decision and he was beginning to think she was dragging her feet.

"Listen, Di. I owe my mother something. I owe her quite a bit, in fact. I wasted a lot of time trying to figure out what life was about and what my place was in the general scheme of things. By the time I'd sorted it all out, I was back where I'd started. But by then, I realized family was more important than anything else. And I needed to make up for some things with mine. So that's why I came back. Unfortunately they're in more trouble than I can easily deal with. But this, at least, I can do for her. I can let her have her party. And she needs help to do it."

Diana listened to him and agreed with just about everything he said. He was a good son after all. And she knew she could help. She sighed.

"All right, Cam. I'll go to see your mother." She shook her head. "But I can't go tomorrow. I've got a doctor's appointment in the morning and I won't be back in time."

"Here in town?"

"No." She looked at him speculatively, then amplified a bit. "I decided from the first that I'd better go to a clinic down in Sacramento. I found a good doctor there. And I didn't want everyone in town knowing all about my pregnancy."

He nodded. "Probably a wise move," he said.

"So I'll plan to come by and see her Friday," she went on. "I'll talk to her." She winced. "But I'm afraid I'm only going to disappoint her."

He grunted and she couldn't tell if he was agreeing with her or dissenting.

"I still don't feel comfortable being a part of the great wife search," she told him, "especially if you plan to thwart your mother on it. If you really mean it, that you won't marry anyone, I hope you're planning to tell her the truth from the beginning."

"She knows how I feel."

"Does she?" Somehow, doubts lingered. "Cam, let's be honest. Your mother is looking for a bride for you, like it or not. It's not exactly fun for me to be a part of that."

"Why is that?" He gazed challengingly into her eyes. "Tell me what bothers you about that?"

Her lower lip came out. "You know very well what it is," she said in a low, grating voice. "It's not really fair of you to make me say it. You know exactly what it is and you know there's no cure for it."

With that, she grabbed her map and slipped out of the car, heading for her little lonely house.

Cam sat for a long time, not moving, not reaching for the ignition, just staring at the moon. And then, finally, he headed home.

CHAPTER EIGHT

DIANA dreamed about Cam, about his kiss and how lovely it was to be in his arms. And then she woke up and there he was on her doorstep.

"Doughnuts," he said, holding out a sack of them like a peace offering. "For your breakfast."

"Thank you," she said, taking the bag and closing the door right in front of him.

"Hey," he protested, and she opened the door again, pretending to scowl at him.

"Too early," she said. "You're not even supposed to see me like this."

"I'll close my eyes," he lied. "I came early because I didn't want to be too late to take you to the doctor."

She stared at him, and slowly, she opened the door wider for him to come in. Turning, she looked up at him. "I don't need anyone to take me to the doctor," she said stiffly.

"I'm not trying to horn in on your private business," he assured her. "In fact, if you want me to, I'll wait in the car. But I think you ought to have someone with you, just in case. And since the baby's father isn't around to help you, you can count on me. I'll be around in case something happens, or whatever."

You can count on me—the words echoed in her head. She knew he meant it, but she also knew he couldn't promise anything of the sort. "Cam, I really don't need help."

He stared down into her wide eyes. "Yes, you do," he said firmly. "Di, I know you can do this on your own. You're very brave and you've tried your whole life to do everything on your own. I know you don't actually, physically, need any help. You're strong. You've done it all on your own forever."

Reaching out, his hands slid into her hair, holding her face up toward him. "But everyone needs somebody. No one can chart his own course forever. I'm here now. I can help you. I can give you some support and be around in case you need a shoulder to lean on. You don't have to be alone."

To her horror, her eyes were filling with tears. She fought them back. The tears were a sign of weakness, and she couldn't afford to show that side to anyone. But as she fought for control, he was kissing her lips, moving slowly, touching gently, giving comfort and affection and a sense of protection that left her defenses crumbling on the floor. She swayed toward him like a reed in the wind. He was so wonderful. How could she resist him? A part of her wanted to do whatever he said, anytime, anywhere. And that was exactly the part she had to fight against.

He pulled back to look at her, his gaze moving slowly over her face, a slight smile on his own.

"Please, Diana," he said softly. "Let me be there for you. I'm not asking for anything else. Just let me be there."

She was really crying now. Deep sobs were coming up from all her past pain, all her loneliness, and she was helpless in his arms. He pulled her up against his chest and stroked her hair. When she could finally speak again, she pulled back and looked at him. How was she going to make him understand?

"Cam, don't you see? I can't start to depend on you. If I do that…"

"I'm not asking for a long-term commitment and I'm not offering one," he insisted, holding her loosely, looking down into her wet, sleepy face and loving it. "But I am here now. I can help you. You could use a friend. I want to be that friend. That's all."

She closed her eyes. Didn't he understand how dangerous this was for her? Didn't he see how much she loved him? She had to send him away. It was the only chance she had for strength and sanity.

She felt him move to the side and heard paper rustling and she slowly opened her eyes and then her mouth to tell him to go, but before she got a word out, he popped a piece of doughnut inside it.

"Let's eat," he said cheerfully, and his comical look made her laugh through her tears. She chewed on the delicious confection and laughed at his antics and somehow her resolutions got forgotten for the time being.

But she knew this wasn't the end of the matter. She

might let her guard down for now, but very soon, she would have to erect it again. She knew that from experience. So she would let him come with her to her doctor's appointment and she would be with him for another day. And she would love doing it. But it couldn't last and she couldn't let herself be lulled into thinking that.

"If I were one to sing old Elvis songs," Diana muttered to herself the next afternoon. "I'd be singing that 'caught in a trap' song right now."

She was going to help Cam's mother. She'd always known, deep down, that she would end up doing it. The mystery was why she'd tried to fight it for so long. A lot of needless Sturm und Drang, she supposed. She was a pushover in the end.

"You're completely spineless, aren't you?" she accused herself in the hallway mirror. "Shame on you!"

Mrs. Van Kirk had looked so pathetic lying back on her chaise lounge overlooking her rose garden, and she'd been so complimentary about Diana's talents on all scores—and when you came right down to it, Diana liked her a lot. She felt sorry for her, wanted to help her have her silly parties, wanted to make her happy. So in the end, she agreed to take over all the planning for the event. She was to be totally in charge of it all.

So now she was enlisted to help find Cam a bride— what fun.

There was still the problem of how she would be paid. She'd assumed Cam was serious when he'd teased her about doing it for free, but he assured her she would be paid for her work—someday.

"How's this?" he said. "You'll have the first option on our future earnings."

"What earnings?" She knew he was working hard on setting things to rights, and she supposed there was income from the Van Kirk ranch to throw into the mix, plus some of his funds borrowed from his own business. But it all seemed like slim pickings so far.

He gave her a grand shrug. "We may just go in the black someday."

She rolled her eyes. "Great. I'll be looking forward to it."

"Seriously, Di," he said, catching hold of her shoulders to keep her from running off. "I'm going to make sure you get compensated. Just as soon as I've saved this house and have a little spare cash to take care of things like that."

She looked up at him and barely kept herself from swooning. He looked so handsome, his blue eyes clear and earnest, rimmed with dark lashes that made them look huge, his dark hair falling over his forehead in a particularly enticing way. She could feel his affection for her shining through it all. He was hers—in a way—for the next few days, at any rate. Then, if his mother's plans came to fruition, he would be some other woman's. And Diana would be left with nothing but memories.

"Forget it," she said, shaking her head, pushing away her dour thoughts. "I'm doing this for your mother. And that's it."

Of course, it turned out to be even more work than she'd thought it would be. There was so much to do. The event itself was to be called a Midsummer Garden Party to welcome Cam back to the foothills and from what they'd heard, it was already stirring interest all over the valley and environs far and wide.

"Everyone from the Five Families will be attending," Mrs. Van Kirk told her matter-of-factly.

Diana knew who the Five Families were and it made her cringe a little. The Van Kirks were one of those five, though they might be clinging to that distinction by their fingernails at the moment, hanging by the thread of their past reputation. They were all descendants of five Kentucky miners who'd come here together in the nineteenth century as forty-niners, discovered gold in these hills, settled the land and established the town of Gold Dust. They were the aristocracy of the area now, the movers and shakers of local affairs all through the valley, the main landowners and definitely the richest people around.

It was only natural that Cam's mother wanted him to marry one of the young women from that group. Why not? Not only did they have the money, they had the background to rule the area. And Cam was a natural leader as far as that went. So here she was, working hard to help him take his rightful place—at the top of the social ladder and right beside some simpering debutante.

Well, maybe she wouldn't be simpering. In all fairness, the women from the Five Families spent a lot of time doing charity activities and working on cleaning up the environment. But still, they were eligible to marry Cam and she wasn't. So a little resentment didn't seem so out of line, did it?

But she had to shove that aside and concentrate on the work at hand. Establishing a theme came first. They needed something that would allow them to make cheap, easy party dishes instead of the gourmet selections that had been the choice when the fancy chef was being engaged.

She gathered Cam and Janey together and the four of them brainstormed and what they finally came up with was a Hawaiian theme.

"Hawaiian?" Janey wailed. "That's so retro."

"Exactly the point," Diana said. "That way we don't have to spend money on fancy decor items. We can use flowers from both your gardens and my fields. We'll string leis as party favors and have flowers to clip in the hair of ladies who want that. We'll have rose petals floating in the pool."

"But the food," Janey moaned.

"Don't worry, it'll be fine—very colorful and much cheaper. Things like bowls of cut up fruit will serve two purposes—decorating as well as eating. And as for the more substantial items, I have a friend, Mahi Liama, who runs a Polynesian restaurant in Sacramento. I'm sure he'd do a lot of the food for us. Maybe some pit roasted pork and chicken long-rice and poi. The rest will be mostly finger food that we're going to be fixing ahead and freezing and popping in the ovens at the last minute."

Janey groaned. "What a drag. I like it when we hire the work out a lot better."

Diana gave her a pasted on smile. "It'll be great. Just you wait and see."

The invitations came next. They couldn't afford to have any printed up, so Diana scavenged up some lovely notepaper she found in the bottom drawer of a beautiful carved desk in the den and put Mrs. Van Kirk to work doing them by hand. That was something she could do sitting down and it turned out she had gorgeous penmanship.

"The trick is to make it look like we are taking advantage of your handwriting skills and creating something unique without letting on that it's an economy measure," she told the older woman.

"Shall I add a little Hawaiian looking flower, like this?" Mrs. Van Kirk suggested, proving to have drawing talent as well.

"Perfect," Diana said, pleased as punch. "These will be so special, people will save them as keepsakes."

Buoyed by all the praise, Mrs. Van Kirk got busy and had a dozen done by noon on the first day.

Diana conferred with Cam about the seating arrangements. It turned out that he had rummaged in the storage sheds and found at least twenty round tables and a huge group of wooden folding chair to go with them, supplies obviously used for parties years ago. They needed cleaning up and some repair, and probably a coat of spray paint, but it seemed doable and he was already on the job.

There was a large patio suitable for dancing. With a few potted plants arranged along the outer perimeter and a few trellises and arbors set up, it could look stunning.

Diana was beginning to take heart. It looked like things were falling into place pretty easily. The whole family was involved, including a few cousins who stopped by occasionally, and despite the whining from some quarters, she generally thought that a good thing.

She was especially glad to find a way to get Janey to help out. Once she remembered that Cam's sister had been quite a musician in her younger days, she knew exactly how she could use her talents.

"Here's what you do," she told her. "I've called the high school. They have a small jazz combo, a pianist and a couple of different choral groups. I think one's a cappella. Hopefully they can do some low-key Hawaiian tunes. Their music director says they need the experience in playing in front of audiences, so I think we could get them really cheap and they could trade off, one group playing during the opening cocktails, another during the meal, another for the dancing, etc. You go talk to them and see what you can arrange. You'll be in charge of picking out the music. It's all yours."

"You know what?" Janey said, actually interested for once. "Adam, the man I've been dating, has a teenage son who does that DJaying thing at dance clubs to make a little extra money. Maybe he would help out."

"That would be great." She made a face as she had a thought. "Just make sure you have right of approval on everything he's going to play first. We don't want any of the raunchy stuff some of the kids like these days."

"Indeed," Janey said, drawing herself up. "Wouldn't fit the Van Kirk image."

Diana grinned at her. "You got it."

And for the first time in memory, Janey smiled back.

They had been working on party plans for three days when Diana got a present she wasn't expecting—and wasn't too sure she wanted. She was out in the garden cutting back a rosebush in order to encourage a few blooms that looked about to break out, when she noticed a strange sound coming from the toolshed. It sounded as though an animal had been locked in by mistake.

Rising with a sigh, she went to the door and opened it. Inside she found a small caramel-colored ball of fluffy fur. The puppy looked up at her and wriggled happily.

"Well, who are you, you little cutie?" she said.

Kneeling down beside him, she pulled out the tag tied around his neck. "Hi," the tag said. "I'm Billy and I belong to Diana and Mia Collins, only they don't know it yet."

"What?"

She rose, staring down at the dog as Cam came into the shed.

"What do you think?" he asked, a smile in his voice if not on his face.

She whirled to meet him.

"*You* did this," she said accusingly.

He put a hand over his heart. "Guilty as charged." He wiggled his eyebrows at her. "A friend of mine had a whole litter of these cute little guys. I picked out the best one for you."

She frowned, feeling frazzled. "Cam, I can't take care of a puppy."

"Sure you can. I'll help you."

She sputtered, outraged that he would take it upon himself to do this to her. He looked at her earnestly.

"Di, calm down," he said. "You know very well you need a dog. This little fellow is going to grow up to be a good watchdog. He'll be there to protect you and the baby when…well, when I can't."

She understood the theory behind the gift. She just wasn't sure she appreciated the motives.

"Cam," she said stubbornly, "if I decided I needed a dog, I could get one for myself. And right now, I don't need a dog."

He didn't budge an inch, either. "You need the protection. Living alone like you do, out there in the sticks, it's too dangerous." He gave her a trace of his lopsided grin. "You never know what sort of madman might show up drunk on your pier in the middle of the night."

She turned away. So that was it. The dog was supposed to take his place. Was he just trying to ease his guilt over the fact that he was not going to be there for her when she needed him in the very near future? She could never have him, but she could have his dog. How thoughtful of him. She was tempted to turn on her heel and leave him here with his bogus little animal.

But she looked down and saw a pair of huge brown eyes staring up at her, a little tail wagging hopefully, a tongue lolling, and she fell in puppy love.

"What am I going to do with you?" she asked the pup.

Billy barked. It was a cute bark. An endearing bark. And it cemented the future for Billy. He was going home with her. There was no doubt about that. Still, there were problems and concerns attached to this gift.

She frowned, biting her lip and thinking over the logistics of the situation. "But I'm over here all day. I can't just leave him alone at the lake, not at this age."

"I agree," Cam said. "That's why I rigged up a dog run alongside the shed. You can have him here with you in the daytime. He'll go home with you at night."

Cam had thought of everything. She looked at him, loving him and resenting him at the same time. Slowly she shook her head. "I don't know what my little black kitten is going to think of this," she said.

"They're both young. They should be able to adjust to each other quickly."

She looked up at Cam. A few weeks before she hadn't had anything. Now she had a baby and she had a kitten and she had a dog. The only thing she still lacked was a man of her own. But you couldn't have everything, could you?

She shook her head, looking at him, loving him. He shrugged, his arms wide, all innocence. And she laughed softly, then walked over and gave him a hug.

"Thank you," she whispered, eyes shining.

He dropped a kiss on her lips, a soft kiss, barely a gesture of affection, and turned to leave before she could say any more.

* * *

It was at the beginning of her second week of work on the party that Diana came face-to-face with Cam's grandfather for the first time. She'd been working hard on all aspects of the preparations and she'd gone into the house to get out of the sun and found herself in the cool library with its tall ceilings and glass-fronted bookcases. It felt so good, she lowered herself into a huge leather chair and leaned back, closing her eyes.

At times like this she was getting used to communing silently with baby Mia, giving her words of encouragement, teaching her about what life was going to be like once she emerged from her protected cave and came into the real world. She knew the baby couldn't really hear her thoughts, but she also knew that something was communicated through an emotional connection that was getting stronger every day. Hopefully it was the love.

The minutes stretched and she fell asleep, her hands on her rounded belly. The next thing she knew, there was an elderly man standing over her, peering down as if to figure out who she was and just exactly why she was sleeping in his chair.

"Oh!" she cried, and she jumped up as smoothly as she could with the extra weight she was carrying. "I'm sorry, I…"

"Sit down, sit down." He waved his cane at her sternly. "Just sit down there and let me look at you, girl."

She glanced toward the exit, wishing she could take it, but reluctantly, she sank back down into the chair and tried to smile. She knew right away who this was, and if she hadn't known, she would have guessed. She could see hints lurking behind the age-ravaged face of a man who had once looked a lot like Cam, blue eyes and all.

"So you're Jed Collins's daughter, are you?" he growled. "You sure do look like your mom. She was one of the prettiest gals in the valley in those days."

"Th…thank you," she said, still unsettled by this chance encounter. "I think."

He nodded. "She ran off when you were a little one, didn't she? Ever find out what happened to her?"

Diana bristled a bit at the sense that he seemed to think he had a right to delve into her family matters at will. But she reminded herself that he probably thought of himself as a sort of elder statesman of the community, and she held back her resentment, shaking her head. "No, sir. Never did."

"You ought to get Cam to look for her. He could find her. That boy can do just about anything."

"I don't want to find her."

He stared at her for a moment and then gave a short shout of laughter.

"You're as tough as she was, aren't you? Good. Your dad was weak and he couldn't hold on to her. But who'd have thought she was tough enough to go off and leave her baby girl behind like she did? I'm telling you, nobody expected that one."

His casual assumptions outraged her. Who did he think he was to make these judgments on her family members? And yet, he was bringing up issues no one ever dared talk about in front of her. So in a way, it was sort of refreshing to get things out in the open. She'd never really had a chance to give her thoughts on the situation before, with everyone tiptoeing around it. Now was her chance, and she took it.

"You call that being tough?" she challenged, trying to ignore the lump that was rising in her throat. "For a woman to leave her six-year-old daughter behind in the care of a man who had no ability to handle it?" Her eyes flashed with anger, and that was reassuring. She would rather have anger than tears. "I call it being selfish and cruel."

He reared back and considered what she had to say as though he wasn't used to people disagreeing with his proclamations.

"Well, you would I suppose. But you don't know why she did it, do you? You're judging results, not motives."

She drew in a sharp breath. "You're darn right I'm judging results. I'm living the results."

He chuckled. "You've got fire in you, I'll say that," he said gruffly. "I know that grandson of mine has always had a special place in his heart for you." He frowned, looking at her. "But we all have to make sacrifices."

"Do we?"

"Damn right we do." He waved his cane at her again. "He promised me years ago he would marry one of the gals from the Five Families. I had everything set up and ready to go when he lit out on me. Left that poor little girl in the lurch."

He stamped his cane on the ground and suddenly he looked exhausted, leaning on it.

"Now he's going to have to make up for it." He shook

his shaggy head. "He's a good boy. I knew he'd come through in the end. Not like his worthless father."

Diana stared at him. This was all news to her. "Cam was set to marry someone when he left ten years ago?" she asked softly, heart sinking. That would explain a lot. And make things murkier in other ways.

"Darn right he was. Little Missy Sinclair. Now he'll finally get the job done."

Cam appeared in the doorway before the old man could go on with his ramblings.

"Here you are," he said to his grandfather. "I didn't know you'd come all the way downstairs." He threw Diana a glance as he came up and took the old man's arm. "Come on. I'll help you back to your room."

"I'm okay, I'm okay," the older man grumbled. "I've just been talking to the Collins girl here. Pretty little thing, isn't she? Just like her mama."

"That she is," Cam agreed with a grin her way. "And the more you get to know her, the more you're going to like her."

"Well, I don't know about that," he muttered as his grandson led him away. "We'll see, I suppose."

Diana sat where she was as they disappeared down the hallway. She would wait. She knew Cam would come back down to talk to her. And she had some things she wanted to talk about—like secret engagements and leaving people in the lurch.

She looked up as he walked back into the room.

"Sorry about that," he told her with a quick smile. "He usually doesn't come downstairs these days. I hope

he didn't say anything…well, anything to upset you."
His gaze was bright as he looked at her and she had the
distinct impression he was afraid exactly that had
happened. And in a way, he was right.

"He did say something that surprised me," she told
him, wishing her tone didn't sound quite so bitter, but
not knowing how to soften it right now. "I didn't know
you were supposed to marry someone just before you
ran off to join the circus ten years ago."

He sat down on the arm of her large leather chair and
shook his head as he looked down at her. If her use of
that phrase for his leaving didn't show him that she still
harbored a grievance from those days, her tone would
have given him a clue.

"Di, come on. I didn't run off to join the circus."

"Well, you might as well have." She bit her lip, realizing she was revealing a reservoir of long pent-up anger
against him for doing what he'd done and leaving her
behind. Just like her mother had. Funny, but she'd never
connected those two events until today, when Cam's
grandfather had forced the issue.

"There were a lot of reasons behind my leaving at the
time," he told her, taking her hand up and holding it in his.

This was all old news as far as he was concerned.
He'd thought she understood all this. Of course, he had
to admit, he'd never told her about the arranged
marriage that never happened—mostly because he'd
always known he wouldn't go through with it. And so
had the so-called "bride." It had never been a major
issue in his thinking—except to avoid it.

"Mostly I needed to get out from under the suffocating influence of my grandfather. And part of what he was trying to force on me was a marriage to a girl I had no interest in marrying. But that was just part of it."

She nodded, digesting that. "Who was she?"

He hesitated, thinking. "Tell you the truth, I forget her name."

"Missy Sinclair?"

He looked at her penetratingly. "If you knew it, why did you ask?"

She shrugged. The turmoil inside her was making her nauseous. "Did you ask her to marry you at the time?"

"No." He began to play with her fingers as he talked. "It wasn't like that. Me marrying Missy was cooked up between my grandfather and Missy's grandfather about the time she was born. I had nothing to do with it and never actually agreed to it. Never."

Diana took in a deep breath, trying to stabilize her emotions. "Where is she now? Is she still waiting?"

"Are you kidding?" He laughed and went on, mockingly. "Selfish girl. She couldn't wait ten years. She went ahead and married some guy she actually loved. Strange, huh?"

She finally looked up and searched his blue eyes. "You didn't love her? Not even a little bit?"

He pressed her fingers to his lips and kissed them, holding her gaze with his own the whole time. "No, Diana, I didn't love her and she didn't love me. It was our grandfathers who loved the idea of us getting married. We both rebelled against it. The whole thing was dead on arrival from the beginning. The only one who even remembers the agreement is my grandfather. Forget about it. It meant nothing then and means nothing now."

She closed her eyes. She really had no right questioning him about this. What did she think she was doing? He had a right to get engaged to anyone he wanted. She had no hold on him, even though the things he did could hurt her more deeply than anything anyone else alive could do.

If only she had followed through on her original intention to stay away from Cam. Now it was too late. She was heading for heartbreak on a crazy train and there was no way to get off without crashing.

CHAPTER NINE

BABY MIA was moving all the time now. Diana was bursting with joy at the feeling. The tiny butterfly wing flapping sensations had grown into full-fledged kicks. She would feel Mia begin to move and she would bite her lip and her eyes would sparkle and she would think, "There you go, little girl! Stretch those little legs. You'll be running in no time."

It was hard feeling like she couldn't tell the people around her what was happening. One afternoon, she couldn't contain it any longer. Mia was kicking so hard, it was making her laugh. She sidled up to Cam, who was overseeing some workers who were building a trellis and whispered to him.

"Give me your hand."

He looked at her, surprised. He'd just come back from a meeting with some bankers, so he was in a business suit and sunglasses and looking particularly suave and sensational. But he did what she asked, and she placed his hand right on the pertinent part of her tummy.

He stood very still for a moment, then turned to her with wonder in his eyes.

"Oh my God. Is that…?"

"Yes." Her smile was all encompassing. "Isn't it funny?"

He stared at her, his blue eyes luminous. "It's like a miracle."

She nodded, filled with joy. He took her hand and pulled her behind the gazebo where they could have a bit of privacy.

"How amazing to feel a new life inside you," he said, flattening his hand on her stomach again with more hope than success. "Di, it's wonderful."

"I can't tell you how transporting it is," she agreed. "It's really true. I'm like a different person."

His smile grew and took in all of her. "No," he said, cupping her cheek with the palm of his hand. "You're the same person. You just have new parts of you blossoming."

She nodded happily. Impulsively she reached up and kissed him, then turned quickly and retreated, back to work. But his reaction had warmed her to the core. She loved her baby and having him appreciate that, even a little bit, was super. Just knowing she had her baby with her was enough to flood her with happiness. All the worries and cares of the day fell away as she concentrated on the baby she was bringing to the world.

She had some qualms about raising Mia alone, without a father figure to balance her life. She'd gone through a lot of soul searching before she'd taken the plunge into single motherhood. Was it fair to the child?

Would she be able to handle it? She knew she was taking a risk and that it would be very hard, but she also knew she would do what was best for her baby, no matter what. And once she'd taken the step, she hadn't looked back for one minute.

She'd begun to buy baby clothes and to plan what she was going to do with the second bedroom in her house, the one she was converting into a nursery.

"I'll paint it for you," Cam had offered. "You shouldn't be breathing in those paint fumes while you're carrying Mia."

She'd taken him up on that offer and they had spent a wonderful Saturday trading off work and playing with Billy and the kitten. While Cam painted the room pink, Diana made chocolate chip cookies and worked on a pet bed she was constructing for the puppy.

Afterward, they took fishing poles out to the far side of the lake and caught a few trout, just like they had in the old days, catch and release. Diana made a salad for their evening meal and afterward, Cam found her old guitar and sat on the couch, playing some old forgotten standards and singing along while she watched.

A perfect day—the sort of day she would want for her baby to grow up with, surrounded by happiness and love. If only she could find a way to have more of them.

She walked him out to his car as he was leaving. The crickets were chirping and the frogs were croaking. He kissed her lightly. She knew she shouldn't allow it, but it was so comforting, so sweet. She leaned against him and he held her loosely.

"What would your father say if he could see you now?" he wondered.

She thought for a moment. "If he could see me now, he'd be out here with a shotgun, warning you to go home," she said with a laugh.

"You're probably right," he said. "Maybe it's just as well he's gone."

"I do actually miss him sometimes," she said pensively. "And I know I'm going to wish he could see Mia once she's born."

"Better he's not here to make her life miserable, too," Cam said cynically.

She sighed, knowing he was right but wishing he wasn't. If only she could have had a normal father. But then, what was normal anyway?

"He apologized to me toward the end, you know," she told him.

"Did he?"

She nodded. "He told me a lot of things I hadn't known before, things that explained a lot, things about his own insecurities and how he regretted having treated my mother badly. It's taken me some time to assimilate that information and assign the bits and pieces their proper importance in my life. Just having him do that, filling in some gaps, put things into a whole new perspective for me."

"No matter what his excuses, it can't justify what he did to you," Cam said darkly. Anger burned in him when he remembered how those bruises had covered her arms at times.

"No, I know that. I want to forgive him, but it's hard. It's only been very recently that I've even been able to start trying to understand him…and my mother…and what they did."

He held her more closely. "You deserved better parents."

She sighed. "I'm trying to get beyond blaming them. In a way, they only did what they were capable of doing."

He didn't believe that, but he kept his dissent to himself. If she needed to forgive them to make her life easier, so be it. He had no problem with that. He only knew that *he* didn't forgive what they'd done to her and there was a part of him that would be working to make it up to her for the rest of his life.

Billy began to yip for attention back in the house. They laughed.

"I guess I'd better get going," he said.

He looked at her from under lowered lids, looked at her mouth, then let his gaze slide down to where her breasts pushed up against the opening of her shirt. His blood began to quicken, and then his pure male reaction began to stir, and he knew it was time to go.

She nodded, but she didn't turn away.

He wanted to kiss her. He wanted to do more than that and he knew it was folly to stay any longer. Steeling himself, he let her go and turned for the car. Reaching out, he opened the door, but before he dropped inside, he looked back. And that was his fatal error.

One look at her standing there, her hair blowing around her face, her lips barely parted, her eyes full of something smoky, and he was a goner. In two quick steps he erased the space between them, and before she could protest, he was kissing her, hard and hot.

She didn't push at him the way he thought she would. Instead her arms wrapped around his neck and she pressed her body to his. He kissed her again and this time the kiss deepened.

She drank him in as though he held the secret of life, and for her, in many ways, he did. His mouth moved on hers, his tongue seeking heat and depth, and she accepted him, at first gladly, then hungrily, and finally with nothing but pure sensual greed.

This was what he'd been waiting for, aching for, dying for. All the doubts about who she might really want in her life dried up and blew away. He had her in his arms and that was where she belonged. He was going to stake a claim now, and if any other man wanted to challenge it, he'd better bring weapons.

Diana gasped, writhing in his embrace and wondering where this passion had come from. It had her in its grip, lighting a fire inside that she'd never known before. Every part of her felt like butter, melting to his touch. She knew this was crazy, this was playing with fire, but she couldn't stop it now. She wanted more and she wanted it with a fever that consumed her.

Billy barked again, and just like that, the magic evaporated, leaving them both breathing hard and shocked at what they had just been through.

"Oh my," Diana said, her eyes wide with wonder as she stared at him.

"Wow," he agreed, holding her face with two hands, looking down into her eyes as though he'd found something precious there.

"You...you'd better go," she said, stepping back away from him and shaking her head as though that would ward off temptation.

He nodded. "Okay," he said reluctantly, his voice husky with the remnants of desire still smoldering. He didn't dare touch her again, but he blew her a kiss, and then he was in his car and gone.

Diana watched him until his taillights disappeared around the far bend. Then she bit her lip and wondered why she seemed to be into torturing herself.

"The more greedy you get," she told herself, "The more you're going to miss him when he's gone."

But she had to admit, right now, she didn't really care. Right now she had gathered another memory to live with. And she would surely hold it dear.

The work was going well and the party was only a couple of days away. Janey had thrown herself into picking the musicians and the music, auditioning all sorts of groups as well as the high school kids. Every spare moment was filled with food preparation, mostly of the finger food variety—lumpia, teriyaki chicken wings, pineapple meatballs, tempura shrimp, wontons and everything else they could think of. Rosa set out the ingredients and Diana and Janey began to cut and mix. Rosa manned the ovens. Janey cleaned the trays. And once each batch was cooked, it was filed away in one of the massive freezers the estate maintained.

Meanwhile Mrs. Van Kirk was busy going through the RSVP returns and setting up place cards for the tables.

"The Five Families are coming en masse," she announced to everyone, happily running through her cards. "The eligible young woman count is at eleven and rising fast. Once they find out Cameron is up for matrimonial grabs, they sign up without delay. He's quite popular among them, you know."

Diana didn't have to be told. She already knew and she was sick at heart about it. She knew this was the last gasp as far as her relationship with Cam went. His family wanted him to marry a rich lady and that was what he was going to have to do. He might not know it yet, but she did.

He felt guilty for leaving his family in the lurch ten years before. He was ready and ripe for the picking as far as expiating that guilt and doing what would make his family happy and solvent went. He was going to have to marry someone. He just hadn't faced it in a calm and rational way.

Her mind was made up. She was going to endure this party to the best she could and then she was going to head home and stay away from the Van Kirks for the rest of her life. Every one of them. She would have Penny come and do the weekly flower arrangements and she herself would have no further contact with these people. That was the only way to preserve her happiness and her sanity. It wasn't going to be easy, but she would keep her allegiance to her baby uppermost in her mind and she would fight through the pain. It had to be.

Cam sat in his car staring at the Van Kirk mansion. He'd been in Sacramento doing some research and he had some news for Diana, who was inside, working on party preparations. He wasn't sure how she was going to take it. He wasn't sure how he took it himself.

His grandfather had mentioned the fact that Di's mother left her at a young age and that no one knew exactly why she might have done such a thing. Was she running off with another man? Had she reached the end of her rope dealing with her drunk of a husband? But if that was the case, why did she leave her child behind? In this day and age, the answers to such questions were a lot easier to find than they had been in the old days before computers and public access to so much government information.

At first Cam had resisted looking into the matter. After all, if Di wanted to know these things, she could have instituted a search herself, years ago. To go ahead on his own was to intrude where he had no right to. And yet, once his grandfather had brought it up, the mystery had nagged at him until he'd had to find out for himself.

His dilemma now was whether or not to tell Diana that he'd done it. And whether or not to tell her what he'd found as a result. What made him think that she actually wanted to know?

But it had to be done. Swearing softly, he got out of the car and started into the house, ready to go looking for Diana. The time of reckoning was at hand.

"Hi," she said, looking harried. "Listen, I need to talk to you. Ben has been calling me."

He reacted quickly to that, turning his head to stare at her. "What for?"

"He wants me to commit to selling out my portion of the inherited land." She appealed to him, a worried look in her large dark eyes. "What do you think? Should I do it?"

He hesitated. He hadn't been able to find out anything that would make him counsel that she turn Ben down, but something about this whole deal didn't seem right to him.

"Maybe you ought to wait," he said.

Diana seemed impatient. "Wait for what? We saw the land. It's not worth much. And I could use the money." She patted her rounded tummy. "I've got a baby coming, you know."

"I know." He smiled at her obvious joy every time she thought of or mentioned her baby. "I've tried to find out if there is any reason he would be so hot to have it, but so far, I haven't found a whisper of anything that would lead in that direction."

He'd come looking for her to tell her what he'd found about her mother, but as he gazed at her now, he thought twice and decided to hold off. She had too many things on her mind as it was. This business about her mother would just add to her worries and she didn't need that. He thought for a moment, then shrugged.

"Oh, what the hell. Go ahead and sell to him. Why not?"

"Okay. I'll give him a call and tell him to write up

his proposal. He said he would send me a check once it was signed." She looked up at him, eyebrows raised in question. "Maybe you could use the money to help with…?"

"Forget it," he said, but he grinned at her. "The amount we need is way beyond what you'll be getting. But thanks for the thought. I appreciate it."

She nodded. "Okay then." She noted a worried look in his eyes and she frowned. "Cam, how's the search for funding going? Have you had any luck yet?"

He shook his head briefly and gave her a fleeting smile. "No. With the economy the way it is, no one wants to take a chance."

She hated to see defeat in his face. "What about your business in San Diego? Have you thought about…" She almost gulped before she dared say the word. "Selling it?"

"Don't you think I've tried that?" He ran a hand through his hair, regretting that his response had been a bit harsh. "Of course I've thought about it. I've even put it on the auction block. So far there have been no takers."

"Oh." She was beginning to realize that this was really not looking good. It just might be that the Van Kirks were going to lose their family home and all the land they'd held for over a hundred years.

Funny how that sent a shiver of dread through her. What did she care, after all? These were people who had scorned her and her family all her life, until very recently. While she and her father had scrimped and clawed their way to a bare bones existence, the Van Kirks had lived a wealthy life of ease and comfort.

Or so it had seemed from afar. Once she got to know them better, she realized they had their own problems, their own demons to deal with. With wealth, your priorities changed, but the obstacles were very much the same. Life was no bed of roses no matter what side of the fence you lived on.

"You mean that darned old Freddy Mercury knew what he was talking about?" Cam said when she tried to explain to him how her thinking was running.

"Only if the Van Kirks end up as champions," she retorted, giving him a snooty look. "No time for losers, after all."

He put his forefinger under her chin and lifted it, looking down into her face. "We're going to come out of this okay, Diana," he said firmly. "I promise. Somehow, someway, I'm going to save the family farm."

She couldn't help but believe him. He had always been her champion, after all.

It was two days later that Cam came to her in a hurry just as she arrived at the estate. She'd barely risen from her car when he came rushing up.

"Diana, I need your help," he said without preamble. "Please. Find Janey and get her to take my mother downtown."

"What for?" The request was a little surprising, as Mrs. Van Kirk hadn't set foot off the grounds since her accident.

"Find some excuse. We've got to get her out of here. We've got appraisers and bank people coming to take a look at the house. It'll kill her if she sees that. She'll put two and two together and get…zero."

"Why are they coming?" Diana asked, not too good at putting two and two together herself.

"Why do you think? They want to take measurements and do evaluations." He gave her a dark look as he turned away. "Let's just say the vultures are circling."

That was an ominous thing to say and she shuddered every time she thought of it. But she did find Janey and prompted her to convince her mother to go into town for a bit of window-shopping. The real thing was off the budget for the foreseeable future. She watched as they drove off in Janey's little sports car, Mrs. Van Kirk complaining about the tight fit all the way. Just as they disappeared down the driveway, a limousine drove up and disgorged a group of businessmen who reminded her of a scrum of ravenous sharks.

Cam went out to meet them and began to take them on a tour of the grounds, talking very fast all the while. She wondered just what line of fantasy he was trying to spin. Whatever it was, they seemed to be listening attentively.

It wasn't until he brought them into the house that she began to realize something was wrong. She heard shouting and as she ran toward the front of the house where the noise was coming from, she began to realize it was Cam's grandfather who was causing a ruckus.

Old-fashioned cuss words were flying as she burst into the library where Cam was trying to quiet the older man. The bankers and appraisers were shell-shocked, gathering against the far wall of the room like a school of frightened fish.

"Get out of my house," Cam's grandfather was yelling. "I won't have you bloodsuckers here. I'd rather die than give in to you thieves. Where's my shotgun?"

"Get them out of here," Cam told her as she skidded to a stop before him, pointing to the group of visitors. "I'm going to lock him in here."

She shooed the men away, then turned back. "I'll stay here with him," she heard herself say, then gaped in horror at her own suggestion. The last thing in the world she wanted to do was stay here with this raving madman, but at the same time, she couldn't see locking him in here all alone. He was too old and too honored a member of this family to be treated like that.

"Really?" Cam looked at the end of his rope. "Great. Thanks, Di. I'll make it up to you, somehow."

He took off after the others, locking the door behind him, and Diana turned to look at the grandfather.

He'd finally stopped yelling and he sagged down onto the couch, his face turning an ashen shade of gray. She quickly got a glass of water from the cooler in the corner and handed it to him. He took a long drink and seemed to revive somewhat. He turned to look at her and frowned.

"They want to take my house away," he told her shakily. "I can't let them do that."

"Cam is going to try to fix it," she said, wishing she had more faith in the fact that a fix was possible. "I think these men are just here to gather some data."

He didn't answer and for a moment, she thought he'd

forgotten she was there. Then he turned, gazing at her from under bushy eyebrows.

"Let me tell you a story, girl. A story about family and friendship and history."

She glanced toward the door. Surely Cam would be coming back to rescue her soon. "Well, if it's only a short one."

"Sit down."

He did have a way with words—a strong and scary way. She sat down.

"I'm sure you know all about the Five Families, how our ancestors all worked together to establish a decent community for our loved ones here. Those bonds were still strong back when I was young. Through the years, they've frayed a bit. But two of us remained true friends, me and Jasper Sinclair. Some called our friendship historic. We were the only remaining descendants in our generation of a group of close friends who had struck out together for the California gold fields in the mid-nineteenth century, men who found their fortunes, and founded a pair of towns rimming the Gold Dust Valley."

He shook his head, his foggy gaze obviously turned backward on ancient scenes.

"Me and Jasper, we were raised to feel it our duty to maintain area pride in that culture and history. The other families sort of dissolved for one reason or another. Oh, they're still around, but their kids don't really have the pride the way they should. The Van Kirks and the Sinclairs, though, we've still got that Gold Rush story running in the blood in our veins."

Diana nodded. She knew a lot of this already, and she knew that it was a Sinclair girl that Cam had been expected to marry ten years ago.

"Jasper's gone now, but he had a passel of grand-daughters. I always said, if Cam can't decide on one of those pretty girls, he just ain't the man I think he is. You see, I promised Jasper I would see to it that we kept the old ways alive. Traditions matter. That's what keeps a culture intact, keeps the home fires burning, so to speak."

Diana took a deep breath and made a stab at giving her own opinion on the subject. "You know, in this day and age, it's pretty hard to force that sort of arranged marriage on young people. It just doesn't fit with the way we live now."

He fixed her with a gimlet eye. "Some of those arranged marriages turn out better than the ones people fall into by themselves," he said gruffly. "Look at your own parents. They married for love. That didn't turn out so well, did it?"

Diana had just about had it with his casual interest in giving out his view of her family affairs.

"Mr. Van Kirk," she began stiffly.

But he didn't wait to hear what she had to say.

"Did you know that your dad and my son, Cam's father, were good friends back before the two of you were born? Drinking buddies, in fact."

That stopped her in her tracks. "No," she said softly. "No, I didn't know that."

He nodded solemnly. "I used to blame him. Your dad, I mean. But now I realize they were both weak, both with addictive problems. Funny, isn't it?"

"Tragic is more like it," she said, but the words were under her breath and he didn't hear them.

He glared at her. "Anyway, I just hope you understand that Cam has got to marry one of them girls. There's no other way. It's either that, or we are over as a family." He shrugged as though dismissing her. "Sorry, but that's the way it is."

Cam returned before he could go on and she rose gratefully, leaving him to take his grandfather back up to his room. She felt numb. She knew what the old man had been trying to say to her. He needn't have bothered. She knew Cam would never marry her. As far as he was concerned, she was pregnant with another man's child. Besides, he didn't want to marry anyone. Didn't the old man know that?

But if all that was true, why was she crying again?

Cam sat in the darkened library staring out at the moon and wondering how things had gotten so crazy. He held a crystal glass filled with golden liquid of a certain potent variety and imbibed from time to time. But mostly, he was lost in thought.

It was the night before the party. Everyone had worked long into the evening, and would be back first thing in the morning to finish preparations before the guests began to arrive. Cam felt tired down to his bones, but he knew it was more emotional than physical.

Tomorrow the grounds would be filled with party-goers. A lot of beautiful young women from eligible families would be showing off their pretty summer dresses. Most of them were just coming to have fun, to see friends, to be at a party. But he knew there were certain expectations, mostly from his own family, that he would choose one of them to court. Preferably one of the richest ones, preferably from one of the Five Families. Hopes were high that he would do something matrimonial to save his own family from being kicked out of their ancestral home.

That wasn't going to happen. Much as he wanted to do something to save his family from ruin, he couldn't marry someone he didn't love. And he couldn't stop loving someone he couldn't marry.

He groaned, stretching back in the leather chair and closing his eyes. He should never have let his mother have her way with this party. He should never have let any of them get their hopes up this way.

Janey had actually brought the subject up earlier that day.

"Look," she'd said, waving a paring knife his way as she took a break from fashioning vegetable decorations. "It's only obvious you're crazy for Diana. You don't want to marry any of those women who are coming. I'm not sure you even want to be here with us."

She waved the knife so dramatically, he'd actually stepped back to be sure he was out of range.

"Why don't you just grab Diana and go? Take off for parts unknown. Leave us behind. We'll sink or swim without you."

He shook his head. "I can't do that."

"Why not?"

"Because it turns out, though I tried for ten years to forget it, blood is thicker than water. I'm a part of this family and I do care what happens to it."

Janey looked at him as though he were demented. "You can't just go off and be happy with the girl you love?"

"No."

Janey looked at him for a long moment, then said, "More fool you," but her eyes were moist and she turned and gave him the first hug he'd had from her since they were children.

A part of what complicated things, of course, was that, even if he wanted to go off with Diana, he wasn't sure she would want to go off with him. He knew she had a lot of affection for him, knew that she'd missed him and resented that he had gone off and left her behind suddenly the way he had—and for so darn long.

But why wouldn't she tell him who Mia's father was? He didn't know anything about the man who had fathered her baby. There was only one reason he could think of for that. She must still love him, still hope to get him to return and take up his duties as her child's father. What else could it be? And if that was still her dream, how could he get in the way?

He wished he understood women better. Somehow their thought processes were such a mystery. Just when he thought he'd figured one of them out, he found she was off in outer space somewhere, running on completely different assumptions than he was.

Gina for instance, the woman he'd lived with for a substantial length of time two years before. He'd thought they had the perfect adult relationship—companionship and sex without strings. She was the one who had suggested it and he'd been glad to accept her conditions. Then, suddenly, she wanted to get married. That was a shocker. He very quickly realized he didn't love her and didn't want to spend his life with her. When he explained that to her, she left in a huff.

A few months later, she was back, claiming to be pregnant with his child. He'd felt trapped, threatened, but he wanted to do the right thing. They planned a wedding, but he was in torture the whole time, resenting her, resenting the coming child, and hating himself for feeling that way.

Out of the blue, she died in a car accident. He was even more miserable, sad for her and the baby, tortured with the way he'd acted. He wished he'd been kinder to her.

Then, when the medical reports came in, he found out that the baby wasn't his after all. The confusion that left him in lasted for months. He couldn't even think about dating again. He didn't trust any woman he met. He'd actually begun to wonder if he would ever feel comfortable with a woman again.

Then he'd come home and there was Diana. It didn't take long to realize he was probably in love with her and always had been. The fact that it was crazy and doomed didn't bother him. He was used to life not turning out the way he'd hoped it would.

A sound in the doorway made him open his eyes and sit up straighter. There was Diana, walking slowly into the room and finally spotting him as her eyes adjusted to the gloom.

"I thought you'd gone home," he said.

"I did, but I forgot to put some of the leis we strung together in cool storage. I didn't want to leave them out overnight."

He nodded. "Will you join me in a drink?" he offered.

"No, thanks." But she came close and perched on the arm of the overstuffed leather chair where he was sitting. "I've got to get on home. I just stopped in for a minute."

"I was just sitting here thinking about you. About us."

She sighed. "Cam, there is no 'us.'"

"I've noticed that, Diana. Tell me why that is."

She looked down at him, startled by his tone. "There's a party happening tomorrow that is supposed to result in you choosing a rich bride to save the family," she said crisply. "That pretty much takes care of any 'us' there might have been."

He shook his head and took a sip of his drink. "I'm not buying it, Di. There's a wall between us and I'm just beginning to realize you put it there."

"That's crazy. I didn't invent this commitment you have to your family. It's enshrined in your Van Kirk legacy. It's like a shield carved into your front door. You gotta do what you gotta do."

"No, I don't."

"Yes, you do. You know very well it's what called you back here. You are part of something you can't shake free of. Duty, responsibility, whatever you want to call it. It's part of you and you're going to do what they expect."

He stared at her in the darkness. Was she right? Was he really going to do this thing they wanted of him?

He loved his grandfather with a fierce devotion, but he'd always resented him and his manipulating ways with almost as much passion. The senior Van Kirk had constantly tried to guide his life, but in the past, he'd resisted, sometimes violently. That was what the whole mad dash to shake off the dust of this gold country town in the hills had been all about. So he'd gone off to get out from under his family's rules and make his fortune. And here he was, coming back into his family's sphere and acting like that had all been a huge mistake. Was he really ready to follow his grandfather's wishes this time?

No. The whole idea was insane.

"Diana, I've told you a thousand times, I'm not marrying anyone."

"Really?" She clutched at the hem of her blouse and twisted it nervously. "Well, I think you ought to revisit that statement."

He frowned up at her. "What are you talking about?"

"You made a promise a long time ago, from what your grandfather tells me. And now that your family needs you to put yourself on the line, I think you ought to fulfill that promise." She knew she was beginning to sound a little shrill, but she couldn't help it. Her emotions were very near the surface and she was having a hard time holding them back.

"You need to have a nice little Five Families baby with one of those super rich girls and save the house, save the legacy, save it all. It's your destiny. It's what you were raised to do."

He stared at her, aghast. "You've really drunk the Kool-Aid, haven't you?"

"I've listened to your grandfather, if that's what you mean. And I've realized you're going to hate yourself if you don't do what you've been raised to think is your duty. You can't fight it."

He swore softly, shaking his head, disbelief shuddering through him.

"Just like I was raised to be pretty much the opposite," she went on, her voice sure but a bit shaky. "That's what my father always used to tell me. 'You're just a white trash girl. Don't get no fancy ideas, running around with a Van Kirk boy. That bunch will never accept you.' That's what he used to say. I didn't believe him then, but now I see the wisdom in accepting the truth."

"Truth." He said the word scornfully. "That's not truth. That's someone's fantasy dressed up as faux reality. You've fallen down the rabbit hole, Di. Stop listening to the Mad Hatter."

She almost laughed. "Your grandfather?"

He nodded. "Despite everything, I love that old man." He shrugged. "And you're right, up to a point. I made certain promises. I've got certain responsibilities."

Reaching up, he caught hold of her and flipped her down into his lap, catching her by surprise and eliciting a shriek as she landed in his arms. "But one thing I won't do is marry a woman I don't love," he said. "And you can take that to the bank."

"Cam…" She tried to pull away but he was having none of it.

His body was hard, strong, inescapable and she knew right away she couldn't stop him. But she didn't really want to and when his mouth came down on hers, it felt so hot, she gasped. His ardor shocked her, but in a good way, and very quickly her own passion rose to meet it. The pressure of his mouth on hers was pure intoxication. She sank into the kiss like a swimmer in a warm, inviting whirlpool, and very soon she was spinning round and round, trying to get her head above water often enough to catch her breath, but strongly tempted to stay below where his smooth strength made her giddy with desire.

He'd wanted to do this for so long, his need was an urgent throb that pushed him to kiss her harder, deeper, and to take every part of her in his hands. He plunged beneath her clothes, craving the feel of her soft flesh, sliding his hands down the length of her, sailing on the sensation like an eagle on a burst of wind. In this moment, she was his and he had to take her or die trying.

The top buttons of her blouse were open and his hot mouth was on her breast, finding the nipple, his lips tugging, his tongue stroking, teasing senses cued to resonate to his will. She was writhing in his arms, begging for more with tiny whimpers, touching him as eagerly as he was touching her.

"More," was the only word that penetrated her heat. "More, please, more!"

All thoughts of duty and responsibility were forgotten.

Thought itself was banished. Feeling was king, and she felt an arousal so intense it scared her. She was his for the taking, his forever. Right and wrong had nothing to do with it. He was all she'd ever wanted. The rest was up to him.

And he pulled back.

She stared up at him, panting, almost begging to have him back against her, and he looked down at her dispassionately, all discipline and control.

"You see, Diana?" he said. "There *is* an 'us,' whether you want there to be or not. You can't deny it. And I can't marry anyone else when I want you more than I've ever wanted any other woman."

He set her back on the wide arm of the chair and rose while she pulled her clothes together.

"I'll see you in the morning," he said, and walked away.

Diana sat where she was, shaken to the core and still trembling like a leaf. She was putty in his hands. He could do anything he wanted with her and her body would respond in kind. She was helpless. Helplessly in love.

CHAPTER TEN

PARTY time!

The scene was being set for a wonderful party. Cam had recruited some old high school friends to come help him and they had strung lights everywhere throughout the yard. They had reactivated a man-made watercourse that had been built years before to run all through the gardens, and now water babbled happily, recreating the look of a mountain stream. Cam had even found a way to put lights just beneath the surface at random intervals, so the whole thing sparkled as though it was under perpetual sunlight.

Guests began to arrive at midafternoon. The sense of excitement was contagious and the air was filled with the scent of flowers and the sound of music. Diana knew very few of the people who arrived. Some were cousins of Cam's who had come by to help a time or two in the past few days. But most of the Five Families children went to private schools, so she hadn't had much occasion to cross paths with many of them, and some of the ones she did know didn't seem to recognize her.

One lucky result of the theme was that no one had even suggested she wear a French maid's costume while mixing with the guests as she had feared at the first. The Hawaiian decor meant that she could wear a beautiful long island dress and put flowers in her hair and look just as good as most of the visitors did.

"I can pretend, can't I?" she muttered to herself as she wove her way in and out of the crowd. Still, she was the one holding the tray with the wineglasses, though, wasn't she? That pretty much gave the game away.

"Oh my dear, you look wonderful!" Mrs. Van Kirk approved, nodding as she looked her over. "I love the garland of flowers you've put in your hair. You look like a fairy princess."

Mr. Van Kirk, Cam's father, was home on a rare visit, looking half soused, but pleasant. He nodded agreement with his wife but didn't say much, except, "Hey, I knew your dad. He was one of my best friends. God, I really miss those days."

And she didn't linger to hear his stories.

Everyone praised the wonderful stream and the lights and the music and once the cocktail hour began to blend into dinnertime, the food was center stage. Diana was so busy making sure there was enough and the access was ample that she hardly had time to notice anything else, but she did see Cam once in a while, and every time her wandering gaze found him, he was surrounded by women.

"I'm sure he's having the time of his life," Janey said, and for once she sounded amused rather than resentful. She had her latest date, Adam, with her. A rather short man, he seemed to follow her dutifully everywhere she went, looking thoroughly smitten, and she seemed to enjoy it.

While she was filling the punch bowl with a fresh supply of green sherbet punch doused with rum and meant to take the place of daiquiris, Janey came up and elbowed her.

"Look at there, by the waterfall. Those three are the prime candidates."

She lifted her head to look at the three beautiful young women. "What do you mean?" she asked, though she was very much afraid she already knew.

"We need Cam to pick one of them to marry. They are the richest ones."

"And the most beautiful, too," she said, feeling just a bit wistful.

"Well, the one on the right, Julie Ransom, is only semibeautiful," Janey opined. "But she's got a wonderful personality."

"Oh, great. Better and better."

"What do you care? He's got to pick one of them."

"I know."

"Tina Justice, the redhead, is said to be a bit on the easy side, but nice. And Grace Sinclair, the one in the middle, is the younger sister of Missy, the one Cam was supposed to marry years ago. She's considered just about the most beautiful woman in the valley. Wouldn't you agree?"

"Oh, yes," she said, heart sinking as she looked at the woman who was wearing a turquoise sari and standing out in the crowd. "She's got that luminous quality."

"Yes. And I think Cam likes her pretty well. So let's work on getting the two of them together. Agreed?" Janey gave her an assessing look, as though wondering how she was going to react to that, but Diana didn't give her the satisfaction of letting on.

"You get busy on that," she said lightly. "I've got some crudités to crunch."

In some ways it was nice that Janey now considered her a coconspirator rather than an enemy, but this sort of scheming put her in a very awkward position. She didn't need it. She was going to keep her distance from actual matchmaking no matter what.

Just a few more hours, she told herself, and then you'll be free. You'll never have to look at this family again. But whether you can forget them—ah, there's the rub.

It was only a short time later that she found herself listening to the three prime candidates as they chatted about Cam, ignoring her completely. She was in the kitchen, taking cheese sticks out of the oven, when they came in to wash a spill out of the redheaded girl's dress at the sink.

"They say his mother is pushing hard to get him to pick a bride tonight," she was saying.

"Tonight?" Grace repeated, looking out the window to see if she could spot him.

"Yes! Have you danced with him yet?"

"Twice." Grace sighed, throwing her head back. "He is super dreamy. I just wanted to melt in his arms. If I can get him again, I'm going to find a way to maneuver him out into the trees so we can have a little make-out time. There's nothing like stirring up the old libido and then doing the old tease for arousing a man's interest in getting engaged. And if his mother is pushing…"

"I haven't had a go at him yet," Julie said with a pout. "You all just back off until I've had my turn."

The redhead frowned thoughtfully. "You know, they also say he's got a pregnant girlfriend in the valley."

Grace nodded. "Could you put up with that?"

Julie tossed her head. "I think I could hold my own against a little piece of valley fluff."

They all laughed and began to adjust their makeup at the kitchen mirror.

Diana looked at them with distaste. She wasn't sure if they'd seen her or not. Somehow she thought it wouldn't have mattered anyway. Thinking her a servant, they would likely have looked right through her. Nice girls.

She gathered some fruit on a platter, preparing to go out with it, but just for fun, she stopped by where they were primping.

"Would any of you ladies like some grapes?" she offered, pointing them out. "They're very sweet. Not a sour one in the bunch."

All three pairs of eyes stared at her, startled.

"No, thanks," one murmured, but it was obvious they didn't know what to make of her. She smiled and carried the tray out into the party area. But her heart was thumping and her adrenaline was up. Nice girls indeed!

The dancing seemed to go on forever. Diana managed to avoid Cam, although she saw him looking for her a time or two. She was not going to dance with him. After tonight, she was going to be a stranger. No sense in prolonging the agony.

Finally the night was drawing to a close. Adam's DJ son had taken over center stage and was announcing themes for dances. It was a cute gimmick and was keeping a lot of people on the dance floor who probably would have been on their way home by now if not for the encouragement from the DJ.

Diana was tired. She wanted to go home and put her feet up.

"The last dance," the DJ was saying on the loud-speaker. "And this one is special. Our host, Cameron Van Kirk, will pick out his chosen partner and then we will all drink a toast to the couple. Mr. Van Kirk. Will you please choose your partner?"

It was like a car crash, she couldn't look away. Which one of the beautiful young women who had come here to look him over and to be looked over would he pick? She peered out between two onlookers and there was Cam. He was searching the scene, scanning the entire assembly, and then he stepped down and began to walk into the crowd.

Suddenly she knew what he was doing. There was no doubt in her mind. He was looking for her.

Her heart began to bang against her chest like a big bass drum and she couldn't breathe. How did she know this? What made her so sure? She wasn't certain about that, but she did know as sure as she knew her own name that he was headed her way.

She turned, looking around frantically. Where could

she hide? He couldn't possibly do this—could he? It would be an insult to all those beautiful, wealthy women for him to pick the pregnant party planner as his special partner. She squeezed her way between a line of people and hurried toward the side exit. And ran right into Cam.

"There you are," he said, taking her hands before she could stop him. "Come with me. I can't do this alone."

"Can't do what alone?" she said robotically, still looking for a chance to escape. But with all eyes on her, she really couldn't push his hands away and she found herself walking with him to the middle of the dance floor.

"Please welcome Mr. Cameron Van Kirk," the DJ said, "and Miss Diana Collins. Give them a hand, ladies and gentlemen.'

The music began and Cam's arms came around her. She closed her eyes and swayed to the music, a hollow feeling in the pit of her stomach.

"You can't be surprised," he said very near her ear. "You know you're my choice. You always have been."

She pulled back so she could look into his face. "I know you think you made a great joke out of this, but…"

"Joke? Are you kidding?" He held her closer. "Diana, face it. I love you."

She closed her eyes again and willed this to be over. She knew he thought he loved her. And maybe he really did. But it was impossible. He couldn't do this.

The music ended and the applause was polite and the toast was pleasant. But people were somewhat puzzled. You could see it in their faces, hear it in their voices. This wasn't one of the girls he was supposed to pick.

Still, people gathered around for congratulations. And while Cam was involved in that, Diane slipped away. She headed for her car. She knew she was being a rat and leaving all the cleanup to others, but she couldn't help it. She had to get away. If she hadn't been here to confuse things, Cam would have been free to choose one of the rich girls. The only remedy she could think of was to clear the field and give him space to do what he needed to do. She had to get out of here.

She raced home, packed a bag in three minutes and called her assistant, Penny, and asked her to come house-sit, kitten-sit and dog-sit. That was a lot of sitting, but Penny was up for it. In no time at all she was on her way to San Francisco. It was going to be a long night.

Cam didn't know she was gone until the next morning when he got an e-mail from her. It was short and scary.

Cam, please go on with your life without me. I'm going to be gone for a week or two so that you can get used to it. When I come back, I don't want to see you. Please. Don't bother to reply, I won't be reading my e-mail. A clean break is the best way. Di.

He went straight to her house just in case and found Penny there.

"She said she had to go to San Francisco," Penny said when he demanded to know where Diana had gone. "I'm not sure where. She'll probably call me tonight to see how the animals are. Do you want me to give her a message?"

He shook his head. "I can't wait until tonight. You really can't give me any better clue than that?"

"Well… She did say something about staying where she stayed when she got pregnant with Mia. I think she wanted to revisit the base of her decision or something. She was muttering and I couldn't really catch her meaning."

His heart turned to stone in his chest. She was going to see Mia's father. He was sure of it. He should leave her alone. Maybe she could work something out with him. That would be best for Diana, best for Mia. Wouldn't it?

Everything in him rebelled at that thought. No! That was crazy. The man was obviously not right for either one of them—and anyway, he wasn't going to give up the woman that he loved without a fight. He was going to find her if he had to go door to door through the whole city.

But first he had to have a last meeting with his grandfather.

He took the stairs two at a time and raced down to the old man's wing of the house, entering his room with a preemptory knock.

"May I talk to you for a moment?"

The old man raised his shaggy head. "I was expecting you," he said simply.

Cam went in and began to pace.

"Grandfather, I've come to tell you that I've failed. I thought I had a line on some financing that might work out, but today I've been told that is no longer an option." He stopped and looked at his aged relative.

"Everything I've tried to set up has fallen through. I've come to the end of my bag of tricks. I don't know where to go from here." Taking a deep breath, he said the fatal words he'd hoped he would never have to say. "I'm afraid we're going to lose the house."

His grandfather frowned. "What about one of the Five Family girls? I saw some that looked interested last night. Don't tell me you're going to turn them down again."

Cam took a deep breath and let it out. "I think you know I can't do what you want, Grandfather. I can't do that to any of those girls. I can't do that to myself."

"Or to the Collins girl," his grandfather said angrily. "Isn't that the real problem?"

He hesitated, swore and turned on his heel toward the door.

"Hold it," the old man called. "Stop right there."

He turned back, eyes narrowed. "Grandfather…"

"You shut up," the older man cried, pointing at him. "I've got something to say."

Cam stood still, his jaw rigid, and his grandfather calmed himself down.

"Now, I know I've been a stickler for staying with the Five Families. Me and the old men of those families— we've always wanted to keep the old times alive by keeping our community together and close-knit. We figured it would be good to get the younger ones to marry in the group and keep us strong. Crazy, probably." Shaking his head, he shrugged. "Time moves on. You can't force these things on people. I know, I've tried to do it often enough."

Cam stood still, scowling.

"What I'm trying to say," the old man went on, "is that I understand. You love the Collins girl, don't you? Even if she's having someone else's baby. Even if it means we'll lose the house. You don't care. You just want her."

"I know that's how it looks to you," Cam said. "And I'm sorry. I've done everything I can to save the house, including putting my own business up for sale. But I can't do what can't be done."

"I know. I know." He sighed heavily. "Oh, hell, go marry your girl. Start over. We'll be okay. We'll get a little place in the hills and live simply. We've gone through hard times before. We can do it again."

Cam felt as though a weight had been lifted from his shoulders. "Grandfather…"

"Just go get her." He waved his gnarled hand. "Go."

Cam stepped forward, kissed the old man on the cheek and turned for the door. He was going to do what he had to do anyway, but having his grandfather's blessing made it so much easier.

Hopping into his car, he turned toward the city by the bay. Just as he was leaving, Penny called on his cell.

"I'm only telling you this because I know she's crazy about you," she told him. "She just called and gave me the number where she's staying. It's a landline. Maybe you can use it to find the address."

Of course he could. And he would.

His research led him to an unassuming row house at the top of a hill. Wearing snug jeans and a big leather jacket, he rang the bell, not knowing whether he would find her with a friend or with the man who'd fathered her baby. When a nice looking young woman answered the door, he was relieved, and it didn't take much fast talking to get past her and into the sitting room where Diana was curled up on the couch, her eyes red-rimmed, her hair a mass of yellow curls around her face.

"I'll leave you two alone," Di's friend said, but he hardly noticed. All he could see was Diana and the wary, tortured look in her dark eyes.

"I love you," he told her, loud and clear. "Di, I want to marry you."

She shook her head. "You can't," she said, her voice trembling. Tears were threatening. From the looks of it, she'd been doing a lot of that already.

He stared at her for a long moment, then looked around the room. "So where is he?" he asked shortly.

She blinked. "Where is who?"

"Mia's father." He looked at her. "Isn't that who you came to find? I want to meet this jerk."

She shook her head. "Why do you call him a jerk?" she asked. "What do you have against him?"

"He went off and left you, didn't he? He's never there when you need him the most."

She closed her eyes and swayed. "Oh, Cam."

He stood right in front of her.

"Diana, there are some things we need to get settled. The most important is whether Mia's father is going to be a part of your life or not. Is he going to be involved in raising her? I don't think you've told me the full truth about the situation yet." He shook his head, his frustration plain in his face. "I want to know who he is. I want to know where he lives. I want to know…if you love him. I want to know what place he is going to have in your life in the future. This is very important."

She raised her face to him. "Why?"

"Because I love you. Don't you get that? And, dammit all, I love Mia, even though she hasn't been born yet. I want to take care of you. I want to be with you. But I have to know…"

She began to laugh. He frowned, because her laughter didn't sound right. Was she getting hysterical? But no. Sobering, she rose from the couch.

"Come here," she said, leading him to a table at the end of the room. "I'll show you Mia's father."

She took out a loose-leaf binder and opened it to a page that displayed a filled-in form. He stepped closer. At the top of the page was the heading, a simple three digit number. Down the page he saw a list of attributes, including height, weight, hair color, personality traits, talents. As he read down the list, his frown grew deeper. It could have been someone listing items about him. Every detail was just like his.

"What is this?" he asked her.

"That is Mia's father," she said, holding her chin high with effort.

He shook his head. "It sounds like me."

She tried to smile. "You got it."

His bewilderment grew. "No, I don't get it."

She took a deep breath. "Cam, Mia's father was a

donor at an assisted reproduction clinic. I don't know him. I never met him. I only picked him out of a book of donors."

"What? That's crazy."

"Yes." She put a hand to her chest. "This is how crazy I am. I went to three different clinics and pored over charts of donors trying to find someone almost exactly like you. I couldn't have you so I tried to come as close as possible to recreating what we might have had together."

He could hardly believe what he was hearing. It sounded like a science fiction story to him. He shook his head as though to clear it. "Diana, I can't believe this."

Tears glittered in her eyes. "Do you hate me? I knew it was nuts. I felt like a criminal doing it. And…I sort of feel as though I was doing it to close that door, stop the yearning. I knew if I was going to do this, it would put a barrier between us that couldn't be overcome. But it didn't seem to matter, because there was less and less hope of ever seeing you again anyway." She took a deep breath and shook her head. "But I just had to go on with my life and stop waiting for you."

"So you got pregnant." He frowned, trying to assimilate this information. "Artificial insemination?"

"Yes."

"And then I came back."

She nodded. "How could I know you were ever going to come back? Cam, it had been ten years. Your family acted like you were dead. I had no way of knowing."

"Oh, Diana." Reaching out, he enfolded her in his

arms and began to laugh. "So you're telling me you're actually carrying my baby. Or a reasonable facsimile thereof. There is no other man involved. Just an anonymous donor."

"That's it."

He laughed again, then kissed her and looked down into her pretty face. "Let's get married."

"Wait, Cam…"

"I mean it, Di. We've already got our baby. All we need is a wedding ring."

"But what about your family?"

Quickly he told her about his conversation with his grandfather. "He basically gave me permission to marry you. Not that I was waiting on that. But it does make it less stressful."

She searched his eyes. "Are you sure?"

"I'm sure." He dropped another kiss on her lips. "Say 'yes'."

She smiled up at him. "Yes."

He whooped and danced her around the room. "I love you so much," he told her. "Last night when I made you dance with me, you looked so beautiful, I could hardly stand it."

"It was a nice party. Even if it didn't get you a wealthy bride."

"C'est la vie," he said, and reached down to pick up some papers that had fallen out of his jacket pocket when he'd danced her around the room.

"What are those?" she asked, her sharp eyes catching sight of her own name on one of them.

He hesitated, then nodded for her to sit down at the table. "I got this information a few days ago but I was holding off on telling you," he said. "You see, I did some research on what happened to your mother."

She went very still. "What?"

"And here's what I found." He spread some papers out in front of her and took another out of an envelope. "She died in a cancer clinic in Sacramento. The date makes it right around the time you were six years old."

Diana stared at the papers. "So what does that mean?"

"It's my guess, from all the records I could find and what I could piece together, that your mother got a diagnosis of stomach cancer and she went away to a cancer clinic where she could concentrate on fighting the disease."

"So she didn't run off with another man? She didn't just decide she hated us and couldn't stay with us anymore?" Suddenly Diana eyes were filled with tears again. "Oh, Cam, I don't know what to think. How do you know this? Why didn't my father ever tell me?"

"My guess is that she thought she would get well and come back and be taking care of you again. She thought she had a chance, but luck wasn't with her. She left because she couldn't take care of you and deal with your father while she was going through that."

Diana's brows knit together. "Do you think my father knew?"

"Who knows what he knew or didn't know. From what I hear, he was in pretty bad shape with the drinking around that time. She might have told him and he might have been too out of it to know what she was talking about."

"Or he might have been that way *because* of what she told him."

"True. I don't suppose we'll ever know the truth." He frowned. "So she had no living family, no one to leave you with?"

"Except my grandmother on my father's side. She was still alive. I spent a lot of time at her house in those days. But she died when I was ten."

"And she never said anything to you about your mother's absence?"

She shook her head. "Not that I remember. I was only six years old, you know. Maybe she told me something that I didn't understand at the time. Maybe she just avoided the issue. People of her generation tend to do that."

"True."

Diana drew in a shuddering breath. "It's going to take some time to understand this," she said. "To really take it all in. It's a relief to know she didn't just run off, but it's so sad at the same time, and I feel like it's sort of unreal right now. Like it's about somebody else."

He was frowning, looking at an envelope in the pile of papers he'd given her. "Wait a minute," he said. "What's this?"

He pulled it out. "Oh, I didn't know this had come. I requested some information from a friend about that land you inherited. The envelope must have been stuck in with this other stuff. I didn't see this before."

He slit it open and began to read. Without looking up, he grabbed her arm. "Diana, you didn't sign that contract with your cousin yet, did you?"

"Yes, I did," she said. "I just mailed it today."

He looked up, his eyes wide. "You've got to get it back. Where did you mail it?" He jumped up from his seat. "Quick! Where is it?"

"I put it outside for the mailman this morning. I doubt it will still be there." She had to call after Cam because he was already running to the front of the house. "What's the matter?"

The mailman was at the next house when Cam snatched the envelope from the box attached to the front of the house where she'd put it. He sucked in a deep breath and leaned against the building. "Wow," he said. "Just wow."

Turning slowly, he made his way back into the house where Diana was waiting.

"What's going on?" she said.

He waved the envelope at her. "My friend in Sacramento came through with some inside info. That piece of land? A major hotel chain is planning a huge resort there. That land will be worth twenty times what your cousin offered you for it. Whatever you do, hold on to that land."

"Wow." Diana said it, too. "Does this mean…I'm rich?"

"Pretty much."

A huge smile began to break over her face. "Then I guess you ended up with a rich girl after all, didn't you?"

He grinned and kissed her. "See? That was my plan from the first," he said. "I just had to wait until you were rich enough to help me save the farm."

"Will this do it? Seriously?"

He shrugged. "Hard to tell. But just having it means there are lenders who will give us extensions they wouldn't give us before. It'll certainly help."

"Good." Her bubbling laughter was infectious. "This is too much. I feel like I'm in the middle of an overload situation. Turn off the bubble machine."

"This is just the beginning," he told her, sweeping her up into his arms again. "You ain't seen nothing yet."

And he gave her a hard, deep kiss to seal the deal.

EPILOGUE

MORNING crept in on little dog feet but it was a cold black nose that woke Diana from her sleep. Then two doggy feet hit the mattress beside her head and she sighed. Those feet weren't really so little anymore.

"You monster," she said affectionately, and Billy panted happily, knowing love when he saw it. "Billy's here," she told Cam.

He turned and groaned, then rose from the bed.

"Come on you mangy mutt," he grumbled. "I'll let you out."

She watched him walk naked from the room, his beautiful body shining in the morning light, wondering how she had managed to be so lucky. All her dreams had come true. Did she really deserve this happiness? He was back in a moment and this time he closed the door with a decisive snap, then turned and reached for her before he'd even hit the bed. Making love was sweet and slow in the morning, warm affection building to hot urgency, then fading to the most intense love imaginable as the sensations melted away.

"That one's going to be our next baby," he said, letting his fingertips trail over her generous breasts.

"You think?"

"I know. I could tell."

"How?

"Magic."

Mia's happy morning voice penetrated the closed door. She was singing to herself.

"She's awake."

"She's awake."

"You stay right here," he said. "I'll get her and bring her in bed with us."

She went up on one elbow as he rose from the bed. "Are you going to tell her?"

"Tell her what?"

She smiled lazily. "That she has a brother coming down the pike?"

He gave her his lopsided grin. "How do you know it's a boy?"

"I can feel it."

He frowned skeptically. "How?"

She smiled as though the world was paradise and she its ruler. "Magic."

He laughed and went to get their child. He agreed. Life was good. And Diana was magic.

**We'll be spotlighting a different series
every month throughout 2009
to celebrate our 60th anniversary.**

Look for Silhouette® Nocturne™ in October!

Travel through time to experience tales
that reach the boundaries of life and death.
Bestselling authors Lindsay McKenna, Cindy
Dees, P.C. Cast and Merline Lovelace join
together in a brand-new, four-book
Time Raiders miniseries.

TIME RAIDERS

August—*The Seeker*
by *USA TODAY* bestselling author Lindsay McKenna

September—*The Slayer* by Cindy Dees

October—*The Avenger*
by *New York Times* bestselling author and
coauthor of the House of Night novels P.C. Cast

November—*The Protector*
by *USA TODAY* bestselling author Merline Lovelace

Available wherever books are sold.

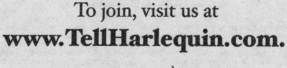

REQUEST YOUR FREE BOOKS!
2 FREE NOVELS PLUS 2
FREE GIFTS!

HARLEQUIN®

Romance®

From the Heart, For the Heart

HR09R

**Stay up-to-date
on all your romance
reading news!**

The Harlequin
Inside Romance
newsletter is a **FREE**
quarterly newsletter
highlighting
our upcoming
series releases
and promotions!

Go to
eHarlequin.com/InsideRomance
or e-mail us at
InsideRomance@Harlequin.com
to sign up to receive
your **FREE** newsletter today!

You can also subscribe by writing to us at: HARLEQUIN BOOKS
Attention: Customer Service Department
P.O. Box 9057, Buffalo, NY 14269-9057

Please allow 4-6 weeks for delivery of the first issue by mail.

IRNBPAQ209

HARLEQUIN *Romance*

Coming Next Month

Available October 13, 2009

Look for the second books in both Marion Lennox's royal trilogy and Barbara Hannay's baby duet, plus makeovers, miracles and marriage, come to Harlequin® Romance!

#4123 THE FRENCHMAN'S PLAIN-JANE PROJECT Myrna Mackenzie
In Her Shoes...
Bookish and shy, Meg longs to be poised and confident. There's more than a simple makeover in store when she's hired by seductive Frenchman Etienne!

#4124 BETROTHED: TO THE PEOPLE'S PRINCE Marion Lennox
The *Marrying His Majesty* miniseries continues.
Nikos is the people's prince, but the crown belongs to the reluctant Princess Athena, whom he was forbidden to marry. He must convince her to come home....

#4125 THE GREEK'S LONG-LOST SON Rebecca Winters
Escape Around the World
Self-made millionaire Theo can have anything his heart desires. But there's just one thing he wants—his first love, Stella, and their long-lost son.

#4126 THE BRIDESMAID'S BABY Barbara Hannay
Baby Steps to Marriage...
In the conclusion to this miniseries, unresolved feelings resurface as old friends Will and Lucy are thrown together as best man and bridesmaid. But a baby is the last thing they expect.

#4127 A PRINCESS FOR CHRISTMAS Shirley Jump
Christmas Treats
Secret princess Mariabella won't let anyone spoil her seaside haven. So when hotshot property developer Jake arrives, she'll stand up to all gorgeous six feet of him!

#4128 HIS HOUSEKEEPER BRIDE Melissa James
Heart to Heart
Falling for the boss wasn't part of Sylvie's job description. But Mark's sad eyes intrigue her and his smile makes her melt. Before she knows it, this unassuming housekeeper's in over her head!

HRCNMBPA0909